SILVER CURLEW

Round the famous old Norfolk story of a little black imp with
a secret name and a twirling tail, who spun twelve skeins of
flax in half an hour to save the pretty head of the Queen of
Norfolk, Eleanor Farjeon has woven a magical story peopled
with memorable characters.

Probably the most important person is young Poll: brown
as a nut; bright as a button; sharp as a needle; inquisitive as a
kitten.

But very important, too, are Nollekins, King Noll of
Norfolk, the king with a double nature, and his sweet Queen
Doll, who loves apple dumplings; and Mother Codling and
her four strong sons; and quiet Charlee Loon, who lives on
the beach and pipes tunes for the puffins to dance to; and the
odd creatures of the Witching Wood, led by old Rackny, and
the Little Black Imp himself.

And always in the background, gliding gracefully along the
wind or swooping to earth like a shooting-star, is the beautiful
and mysterious Silver Curlew.

As a play, *The Silver Curlew* has enjoyed immense popularity
for years. Now, as a full-length, beautifully illustrated story, it
brings new delights for those readers who love both Eleanor
Farjeon and the incomparable Ernest Shepard.

THE
SILVER CURLEW

Eleanor Farjeon

Illustrated by

ERNEST H. SHEPARD

JOHN GOODCHILD PUBLISHERS
WENDOVER

John Goodchild Publishers,
70 Carrington Crescent,
Wendover,
Buckinghamshire,
HP22 6AN.

First published 1953
First published in this new edition 1984
© Copyright Gervase Farjeon 1953, 1984
Illustrations © Ernest H. Shepard 1953, 1984

Cover design by Graham Andrews.

Printed by Nene Litho, Wellingborough, Northants
Bound by Woolnough Bookbinding, Wellingborough, Northants.

British Library Cataloguing in Publication Data
Farjeon, Eleanor
The silver curlew
I. Title   II. Shepard, Ernest H.
823'.912[J]   PZ7

ISBN 0-86391-012-2

To

CLIFTON AND YOMA
who made the magic
when this tale was
acted

Contents

Contents

CHAPTER I

Mother Codling and Her Family

MOTHER CODLING lived in a windmill in Norfolk near the sea. Her husband the miller had been dead for a number of years, during which Mother Codling had kept the mill and her family going. The sails went round, and the corn was ground, and the little Codlings were clothed and fed. The mill-stones turned the red-gold grains of wheat into fine white flour, while time turned Mother Codling's children from babies into little girls and boys; and the fine white flour was changed in the oven to plump loaves of bread, while the girls and boys were changed

I

by the passing years into healthy young men and women.

There were six of them, four boys and two girls. Abe, Sid, Dave, and Hal Codling worked in the fields, ploughing and harrowing, sowing and reaping, all round the year. They were good strong lads with enormous appetites, who said little and thought less. So much for Abe, Sid, Dave, and Hal.

Doll Codling was a blooming wench of eighteen, as buxom as a cabbage-rose, and as sweet. She had a skin like strawberries and cream, hair like a wheat-field in August, and big blue eyes, soft and shining like the summer sea. As well as good looks, she had a good temper and a good heart; indeed, she had only one fault. Doll Codling was as lazy as a sloth, that spends its life hanging upside-down on a tree. Not that Doll did so, or even wanted to. What she liked doing was to sit with her hands in her lap, dreaming about what would happen next. As the next thing that happens is always breakfast, or dinner, or tea, or supper: breakfast-dinner-tea-and-supper was what she dreamed about. That's Doll.

Poll was quite another cup of tea. She was the youngest of the Codlings, not yet grown up, being just twelve years old. She was brown as a nut, bright as a button, sharp as a needle, and inquisitive as a kitten. She had never stopped asking 'Why?' This is a habit all children grow into, and some grow out of; Poll Codling was one of those who didn't. She *wanted to know*, and was restless till she had found the answer; which, as soon as she had found it, started a new question running like a hare. As nobody yet has caught up with the last answer to the last question, Poll was always chasing her hare, and always would be. And that's Poll.

As for Mother Codling, she was at least half as big

3

again as *your* mother, with a body like a sack of flour, arms like roly-poly puddings, and hands like Norfolk dumplings. She was as busy as Doll was idle, which is to say all the time; and she had as few ideas in her mind as Abe, Sid, Dave, and Hal put together, which is to say next-to-none; but she had a tongue that could clack when it wanted to, though what it had to say was of no consequence. She had feelings of sorts for her children, but they didn't come to the surface, and were like stray currants buried in the middle of a suet duff; you might come on them with luck, but most often you didn't. For the rest, she baked and she brewed, she scoured and she scrubbed, she made and she mended, she weaved and she span, she washed, starched, and ironed, she trimmed the lamps, and swept the floor, and chopped the logs, and burnished the brasses, and she kept the mill-sails turning and the mill-wheels grinding, from crack of dawn to fall of night. That's Mother Codling. Her children called her 'Mawther', because they were Norfolk-born in the days when Norfolk had a King. *His* name was Nollekens.

As for the mill, it stood on a knoll in a cornfield that grew to the edge of the sandy cliff. When the big kitchen door stood open, you saw nothing but a clear sheet of gold blowing away to the line of the green sea flowing away to the verge of the blue sky. Some birds and clouds flying overhead, some poppies and pimpernels growing underfoot, and that was all.

So much for Mother Codling's windmill and the world she lived in.

4

CHAPTER II

Dumplings

ONE fine morning Mother Codling stood up to her elbows in dough at her kitchen table, mixing and kneading bread for the week and dumplings for dinner.

Poll was kneeling on the hearth, raking the red-hot cinders in the baking-oven.

Near by sat Doll, with a hank of flax on the spindle of her wheel, and her foot on the treadle. The foot seemed to have gone to sleep, Doll's fingers lay intertwined on her apron, and her eyes gazed out-of-doors at the puffy white clouds sailing lazily over the corn.

'*Mm-mm-mmm*,' hummed Doll's thoughts, like a swarm of bees in the sun. '*Mm-mm-mmm.*'

'Uff! uff! uff!' panted Mother Codling over her mixing-bowl.

'Oo! oo! oo!' wailed Poll, shaking her fingers.

'What's the matter with *you*?' asked Mother Codling.

'Burned my thumb,' said Poll.

'Come you here and I'll flour that,' said her mother.

Poll came and held out her hand, and Mother Codling floured the burn.

'Mawther,' said Poll, 'why do cinders burn?'

'Because they does.'

'Why does flour make it better?'

'Because it do.'

'What's for dinner, mawther?' asked Poll.

'If you rake out the cinders betimes,' said Mother Codling, 'there's dumplings. And if you don't, there's nothing.'

She made short work of her younger daughter's questions. Every question, in her opinion, had a perfectly simple answer, and this being so she couldn't see the need of putting any questions at all. Her answers, however, seldom satisfied Poll's appetite to *know*; they were like crumbs of bread, when Poll was hungry for the whole loaf. Poll went back to the fire and continued to feed the oven. Mother Codling looked across at her elder daughter.

'Now then, idle! quit dreaming,' said she. 'I want that skein spun before next Sunday week.'

Doll gave the wheel a little turn that was almost less than nothing. Mother Codling shaped up her dumplings, and laid the floury balls out on her board.

'There's Abe's,' said she. 'There's Sid's. There's Dave's. There's Hal's. And there's Doll's and Poll's.' She laid another row of dumplings alongside the

6

first. 'There's second helps all round. And that's
the lot.'

'How many's that, mawther?' asked Doll.

'The round dozen.' Mother Codling dusted her
hands one against the other.

'Is that all?'

'Round dozen's ample for anybody.'

'So it may be,' said Doll, 'but there's six of us.'

'There's seven,' called Poll from the hearth.
'Where's your two, mawther?'

'Dawnt'ee know by now that I can't abide dumplings?' said her mother. She began to put her loaves
on the long-handled spatula. 'Shove 'em along to the
back,' said she, 'and leave room for the dumplings in
front.'

Between them, she and Poll settled the big bake in
the oven.

'Now shut the door, child, and mind not to bang it.'

'Why not?'

'Because 'twill make the pastry fall.'

'Why will it?'

'Because it's a fact,' said Mother Codling, tidying
her table.

'Mawther,' said Poll, 'why do dumplings go in little
and come out big?'

'So do little girls,' said her mother.

'Oh,' said Poll. She thought this over and asked,
'How long does it take for a dumpling to grow up?'

'Dumplings 'll always come agen in half an hour,'
said Mother Codling. Then she peered into her bin.

7

'That's finished my flour. I must needs grind some more.' She prepared to go to the mill, calling over her shoulder, 'You Poll! take a creel, run down to the beach, and see if Charlee Loon have catched some flounders. If he have, bring me a good few for my dinner. You Doll! quit dreaming,' said Mother Codling, and took herself off.

Poll jumped up and unhooked a creel from the wall. Doll sat where she was, without lifting foot or finger.

'Doll,' said her little sister.

'Um?' said Doll, her eyes on a creamy cloud.

'What d'you dream about?'

Doll took her eyes off the cloud very slowly, and in a loving voice said, 'Dumplings.'

'Dumplings!' repeated Poll, her own eyes round with surprise. 'You can't *dream* about dumplings.'

'I can,' said Doll simply.

'Dumplings aren't dreamy,' argued Poll.

'Aren't they though!'

'How many dumplings can you dream about at a time?' asked Poll.

'Round dozen,' said Doll.

'Goodness!' cried Poll. 'You'd burst.'

'Give me the chance.'

'I can't even *think* about a dozen dumplings all at once,' said Poll. 'After about five they start pushing each other so I lose count. I say, Doll.'

'Um?'

'How can dumplings *always* come again in half an hour?'

'Ask me another,' said Doll. 'If mawther says they do, they do. She knows.'

'I wish I knew everything in the world,' sighed Poll.

'I wish you did,' yawned Doll. 'Then you'd stop asking questions.'

'Now then, idle!' Poll cried pertly.

'That'll do,' said Doll. 'One's enough in this house. Spinning I hate, and spin I won't.' She gave her wheel a little push.

'Why do you hate spinning?' asked Poll.

'Because I can't. Just take a look at that.' Doll pulled at the flax with her soft clumsy fingers.

'It *is* a bit of a muddle,' said Poll.

'Nobody likes doing what they can't,' grumbled Doll.

9

'Oh, don't they!' cried Poll. 'I can't fly like a bird, but I'd like to. I can't run like a hare, but I'd like to.

I can't jump like a flea, but I'd like to. I can't be the Queen of Norfolk——'

'But,' said Doll, 'you *can* go down to the beach and see if Charlee's got a catch of flounders. Bring big ones,' she called, as Poll reached the door, where the gulls were reeling and screeling overhead.

Poll paused on the threshold to ask, 'Do you dream about flounders too?'

'Mm,' said Doll pensively. 'I could. But dumplings dream best.'

'Me-uuu! me-uuu!' squealed Poll, mimicking the sea-birds in the sky.

Suddenly the shrill squeals were drowned in wild screechings from a flock of birds from another quarter. Their screams rent the air like the tearing of unbleached linen.

Even Doll turned her lazy head to listen. 'The curlews must be flying over the Witching-Wood,' she said.

The two girls listened till the cries died away. Poll still loitered at the door, with a little puzzled frown between her eyebrows.

'Doll,' she said.

'Um?'

'Why do the curlews cry worst when they fly over the Witching-Wood?'

'Ask me another,' said Doll again. But of course what she really meant was, 'Don't ask me any more.'

'Well,' said Poll resignedly, 'I suppose I'll grow up one day. Then I'll *know*.'

She went across the cornfield swinging her creel.

CHAPTER III

Doll's Day-dream

IT's nice to be alone,' said Doll to herself, watching Poll's quick little figure grow smaller in the distance. 'How folk do like to chatter.'

Doll had never been one to chatter. She was too lazy even for that. From where she sat she could hear the creak of the windmill sails going round, and she saw in fancy the little hard grains pouring in at the top and coming out at the bottom as soft as snow.

'Turn about, sails! Grind away, stones!' thought Doll. 'Flour, more flour, more fine white flour for dumplings. Pounds and pounds and pounds of wheaten flour. Dozens and dozens and dozens of big round puffy duffy dumplings.'

She breathed a sigh of rapture at the thought, and lay back against her tall chair with her head lolling to one side, and her sweet red mouth a little open. The curlews were squealing, the mill-sails were creaking, and the mill-stones were grinding through her day-dream; and all the sounds of summer seemed to be murmuring the same thing.

Queen of Norfolk!
Queen of Norfolk!
Queen of Norfolk Dumplings!

Doll's head dropped down to her shoulder, and she woke up with a jerk. She rubbed her eyes and mumbled, 'Queen of Norfolk, oh dear! Who wants to be the Queen of Norfolk?'

'No girl in her senses, say I,' said Mother Codling, coming in from the mill. 'Quit dreamin', Doll. Queen of Norfolk, indeed! The likes o' you don't wed into the Royalty.'

'Mawther, I didn't——' began Doll, but her mother cut her short.

'That's what's wrong wi' you, my girl,' she scolded, reaching down her bonnet from a peg on the door. 'Your noddle's stuffed full of notions above your station. Seein' yourself in cloth of gold and silver, was you, with dimond crowns on your topknot.'

Doll tried again. 'Mawther, I wasn't——'

'And chains of pearls as big as pigeons' eggs,' her mother ran on, 'and trains of ermine fur forty yards long, and gentlemen bowing and ladies kowtowing, and all Norfolk shouting from Cromer to Norwich, "Here comes our Lady Queen, hurrah for the Queen of Norfolk!"' Mother Codling's eyes were sparkling, and she waved her bonnet till the ribbons fluttered. Then she put it on her head, and tying the strings, 'Give over, do, you gurt stoopid,' she said, 'and be content with what you are.'

'Yes, mawther, I will,' said Doll.

'Then I'll go to the baker and bring back the yeast,' said Mother Codling, 'and just you watch the oven till the dumplings be come agen.'

So saying, she trudged off along the edge of the cornfield towards the village, her shoes shuffling up the soft white dust; and Doll was left to her dreaming.

'Come agen, come agen,' mused Doll. 'Dumplings always come agen in half an hour.' And now a real thought entered her noddle, that made her blue eyes brighter, for it was the nicest thought she had ever had. 'If dumplings *always* come agen in half an hour, what harm in eating this lot now? They'll all be come agen by dinner-time. Mawther knows.'

This beautiful thought was enough to make Doll stir her stumps at last. Leaving her idle wheel, she dragged a stool to the hearth, opened the oven door, muffled her hand in her apron, and pulled out the nearest dumpling. It was already bigger than it went in. She tried it gingerly with her white teeth, and gave vent to a sigh of bliss. Bit by bit she nibbled till it was gone. It seemed to Doll that life could never be fuller.

'Queen of Norfolk, bah!' ran her dreamy thoughts. 'Who'd be the Queen of Norfolk?'

Her hand stole once more to the oven door, and fetched out a second dumpling. She ate it slowly to the very last crumb, and then she licked her fingers.

'Who wouldn't be the Queen of Norfolk Dumplings?' thought she. And for the third time her sticky hand crept to the oven door.

CHAPTER IV

Charlee Loon

CHARLEE LOON, who caught the flounders
Mother Codling liked for her dinner, lived in
a little shack on the sea-shore. It was black
and smelt of tar and salt and seaweed, and when I say
Charlee lived in it I only mean that it was *his* shack,
but he himself was seldom inside it. He was oftener
to be found in his boat, mooning on the sea when it
was calm and tossing when it was stormy. Sometimes
he caught things and sometimes he didn't. Sometimes he went out to fish without his nets, and sometimes he forgot where he had set his lobster-pots. But
other times he came back with his nets full of slippery
silvery herrings or flat white flounders. When he had
beached his boat, he usually forgot that he had a shack
to sleep in, and lay on his face on the shingle looking
for amber, or on his back on the sand staring at the
stars. If anybody came along for fish, they could help
themselves. It was all one to Charlee. But as like as
not, even if there was fish in the boat, they would find
him sliding the herring one after another back into
the sea, or laying out the flounders in rows on the
wet sand, where the next incoming wave would curl
over and foam them away. You never knew with
Charlee, any more than you knew what his age was.
Sometimes he looked one thing, sometimes another;

16

and people were as likely to ask, 'Seen old Charlee lately?' as to say, 'Saw young Charlee this maarnin', pipin' to them puffins.'

All the sea-fowl seemed to be Charlee's friends, but the puffins in particular. They were as familiar with him as if he had been himself a puffin, and they liked nothing better than to flap about when he blew on his tin whistle and sang any small tune that happened to stray through his wits. He was sitting now, whistle to mouth, on the end of his boat with his legs dangling, and the sun scorching his skin through the holes in his old jersey. There were so many holes that you would think, if ever he took the jersey off, his white body must be all over brown and gold spots, like a tortoiseshell cat. Three puffins were swaying and hopping to his tune, to an audience of starfish and jellyfish on the sand—an admiring audience, let us hope, but we shall never know.

Charlee took the whistle from his lips, to sing.

> *Charlee Loon*
> *He was borned too soon*
> *Under the horn of the Hunter's Moon.*
> *So soon as he borned*
> *He piped a tune,*
> *And that was the finish of Charlee Loon.*

There he did finish, because one of the puffins came over to him with outstretched wing.

'What's your trouble?' asked Charlee. 'Empty tummy?'

He dipped his hand down into the boat and fished
up a dab. The puffin took it, ducking its head by way
of thanks, and Charlee started on another song.

> *The tide in the sea runs high, runs high,*
> *The tide in the sea runs high,*
> *And who will dry the poor little Pleiades' hands*
> *When the sea falls over the sky?*

Before he could say, Puffin Number Two toddled
up, and held up its foot.

'And what's *your* trouble?' asked Charlee. 'Wet
tootsies?'

Once more he reached down into the boat, and
fetched up a bit of old red sail, with which he dried
the puffin's feet, one after the other.

> *The tide in the sea runs low, runs low,*
(sang Charlee as the puffin toddled away)

Charlee Loon

The tide in the sea runs low,
And who will comfort and cover the shivering sands
Till the sea comes back in flow?

That question was never answered either, for Puffin Number Three was presenting its back to Charlee with a squawk.

'Got a tickle?' asked Charlee, and his long thin fingers poked in among the feathers to find the place. When the puffin flapped off contented, Charlee tried again.

Charlee Loon
Lives under the dune,
He eats his pap with a wooden spoon,
He wakes by night
And he sleeps by noon,
And that is the finish of——

It wasn't, however, for before he could finish a voice on top of the cliff called, 'Char—leee! O—O! Chaar—leee!'

'O—O!' sang out Charlee Loon. 'Poll—eee! Poll—eee!'

Poll came slithering and sliding down the steep soft side of the cliff, and landed in a tumble at his feet.

'Hullo,' she said breathlessly.

'Hullo,' said Charlee Loon.

The puffins made themselves scarce as quick as they could.

Poll picked herself up and scratched the sand out of her hair, trying to remember why she'd come.

'Hullo, Charlee.'

'Hullo then,' said Charlee.

'Oh, I'd said that, hadn't I? Well—hullo. Oh yes. Mawther wants some flounders.'

'Take your pick,' said Charlee amiably.

Poll climbed over the edge of the boat and saw the bottom covered with fish.

'May I take big ones?'

'Did I say take your pick,' asked Charlee peevishly, 'or didn't I?'

'All right,' said Poll, and began to fill her creel with the best of the catch. Overhead the frightened scream of a bird pierced the air, to be drowned in the frightening screech of some animal.

'Hi you! hi you! hi you!' shouted Charlee, scrambling off the boat. Then everything became a scurry and flurry, and straightening herself up Poll saw the queerest creature she had ever set eyes on darting about the beach with a bird in its mouth. The creature was very thin, with wiry black fur sticking up in tufts on its bones; it had a ragged tail, pointed ears, red eyes, and curving steely claws. Between its hideous jaws the struggling bird gleamed like silver.

'You horrid, you horrid! you horrible horrid!' cried Poll, tumbling off the boat to join the chase. Charlee was leaping and flinging his long lean arms whichever way the creature turned, and Poll hemmed it in from behind as best she could. The creature kept jigging this way and that, and tried to slip between them up the cliff, but down came Puffin Number One to flap it away. Then it tried to escape along the edge of the sea, but Puffins Numbers Two and Three cut it off both right and left. Charlee took his chance to corner it, and got the bird between his hands. The creature snarled, let go, and darted through Charlee's legs. Poll made no attempt to pursue it, glad to see it go; as for the puffins, they retreated as soon as they saw the bird in Charlee's hands. Poll ran to look. Charlee was staring down in awe at the silvery plumage and ivory beak and claws. Poll had never before seen any bird like this one. It was lying very still.

'Oh Charlee, is it dead?' she asked in a whisper.

'No.'

'Hurt?'

'Yes.'

'Badly?' asked Poll.

'Bad enough,' said Charlee, 'but not so very.'

'Do you mean it will get better?'

'May do,' said Charlee.

'Why are you looking at it like that?' asked Poll.

''Tis the Silver Curlew,' said Charlee in tones of awe. 'As sure as I live, 'tis the Silver Curlew. Well, I never did.'

'What didn't you ever?' asked Poll.

'Never did I think,' said Charlee, 'to have the Silver Curlew between my hands.'

'What *is* a Silver Curlew?' asked Poll.

The question turned Charlee peevish all in a trice. '*A* Silver Curlew?' he scowled. 'Don't talk such foolishness.' He turned his back on Poll, and continued to feel for the bird's hurt with his bony fingers.

'Now you're cross,' sighed Poll. 'You do get cross so suddenly.'

'Well, you shouldn't talk foolishness,' muttered Charlee.

'I only said a Silver Curlew like you,' said Poll.

'I said nothing of the sort,' snorted Charles. '*The* Silver Curlew, I said. There's just the one, and this is her.'

Poll ventured close again, to watch Charlee's fingers working delicately at the one-and-only Silver Curlew.

'Sorry, Charlee, I didn't know,' she explained, 'and you know, if you *don't* know, you don't *know*, do you?'

'Say no more,' said Charlee Loon, losing his peevishness as suddenly as he had found it.

'What did the Horrid Thing do to her?' asked Poll.

'Broke her wing,' said Charlee, beginning to set it.

22

'Charlee,' coaxed Poll, 'what *is* it about the Silver Curlew?'

Charlee continued to busy himself with the bird, and Poll saw he was in the mood when you mustn't hurry him. Presently he began to speak in a sing-song voice that seemed to come from a very long way off.

'Once upon a time was a Man in the moon. And once upon the same time was a Lady in the moon. The moon was a wondrous place, more wondrous than the world, but one fine night the Man and the Lady looked down and saw the Tower of Norwich. They had never seen the like of that before, and nothing would do but they must go and find it. The Man he just tumbled off the edge of the moon, and got a bump on his head that addled him a bit. The Lady was cleverer, she changed herself into a curlew and slid down the wind, so *she* didn't bump. Thing was, that come to earth she lost her moon-power, and couldn't change back again. This is her,' Charlee ended, in his ordinary voice. 'Now you know.'

'Oh,' said Poll. As usual, knowing didn't seem enough. She hunted round for a question. 'Was the Moon-lady ever so beautiful?'

'More than the evening star,' said Charlee.

'And the Man in the moon, what was *he* like?'

'I don't seem to remember.'

'Oh,' said Poll, and hunted her thoughts again. 'That hideous horrible hateful Thing, what was it?'

'Something out of the Witching-Wood, that was.'

'Would it have eaten her?'

23

'I wouldn't wonder.'

'How awful,' said Poll. She slid in her next question rather slyly. 'What *is* it in the Witching-Wood?'

Charlee frowned. 'Never you mind what that is in the Witching-Wood,' he said. 'You best give the go-by to the Witching-Wood.'

'Why?' asked Poll.

Charlee bent his head over the broken wing.

'Why? why? why?' cried Poll.

'Don't you go being too curious,' said Charlee.

Poll stamped her foot, crying, 'Why doesn't *anybody* answer my questions?' Then she sulked, because stamping in the sand gives you no satisfaction at all.

'Now who's cross all of a sudden?' asked Charlee.

'Sorry,' said Poll. She peered at the bird. 'Is it done?'

'Best I can,' said Charlee.

'Will it ever fly again?'

'May do. There's no telling,' said Charlee Loon. He stroked the wing-feathers lightly. 'That'll want a lot of looking after.'

'*I'll* look after her,' said Poll eagerly. She emptied the flounders out of her creel, and began to line it with the coarse sea-grass that grew in the silver sand at the foot of the cliff. 'I'll take her home with me and give her bread and honey.'

'She'd sooner have raw fish,' said Charlee.

'I'll come and get some for her every day. I'll look after her day and night. I'll light her a candle so she won't be frightened in the dark.'

24

'*She* wants no candle,' said Charlee. 'Sun and star are the Silver Curlew's lights.'

'I'll put clover and meadowsweet in her cage for her to smell.'

'She's no use for those smells,' said Charlee. 'Salt sea and sand is the smells she likes best. Put seaweed in. A shell or so. And always leave her cage-door open, mind.'

'Why?' asked Poll.

'So if she do mend she can fly,' said Charlee.

'Yes, I suppose so,' said Poll. She laid the Silver Curlew in the grassy creel, and climbed carefully up the cliff.

CHAPTER V

King Nollekens of Norfolk

WHILE these things were happening in the mill and on the sea-shore, quite other things were taking place in the palace of the King of Norfolk, whose name, as I have already said, was Nollekens.

The trouble about Nollekens was his nature. In fact, both his natures, for he had two of them. It all depended on which foot he put out of bed first when he got up. If he got out on his right foot he was gay and generous, and full of enthusiastic plans; which, if not always easy to carry out, were always on the

26

pleasant side of things. But if he got out on his left foot, look out for fireworks! He banged about, poked into everything, and flew into tantrums at the least provocation. Nothing was right on Nollekens's left-foot days, and they generally ended in all the servants giving notice. Next day he would be so nice that they took the notice back again. The only one who could really manage Nollekens on his bad days was Nan, his very, very, very old nurse. She had known him from his cradle, and didn't so much manage him as order him. Nollekens took things from her he wouldn't stand from anybody else, and as he was still quite a young king, only twenty-one in fact, he hadn't dropped his habit of hanging on to her apron-strings.

'What's the matter with *you*, Nolly,' she would say, wiping the tears from his eyes, 'is your double nature.'

'I can't help it, can I, Nanny?' asked Nollekens.

'That's as may be,' said old Nan, 'but if you can't, that makes it no better for the rest of us. If you could help it, you could try to mend it.'

'I will try, Nanny, really I will,' said King Nollekens; and he went to the sweetshop and bought up all the toffee-apples, and gave one apiece to everybody.

That was yesterday. Today, as old Nan was sorting the linen-cupboard, she heard a great clatter-and-batter going on downstairs.

'Tch, tch, tch', she clicked her tongue. 'Nollekens at his tantrums again.' She shook her head severely. She was a tiny little woman, which somehow made her severity more severe. Standing on the top of a step-ladder, she unfolded a sheet and shook her head again as it fell to tatters in her hands. 'What we are coming to I do not know,' said old Nan.

The door of the linen-closet flew open and in ran young Jen, the between-maid, with her eyes popping.

'The King wants fresh sheets for his bed,' she gasped.

'He had some only last month,' said old Nan.

'And a pair of pillowslips, please.'

'One's enough for anybody.'

'And, please, a bath towel, and a face towel, and a razor towel, please.'

'Razor towel forsooth! At *his* age!' sniffed old Nan.

'And a tablecloth and table-napkin, and, please, the table-napkin must be sure to match the tablecloth.'

'God bless us! anything else?' inquired old Nan.

'Yes,' said young Jen, 'a clean pocket-handkerchief.'

The bangings downstairs grew noisier and noisier, and the next moment John the Butler staggered in.

'Mrs Nan! Mrs Nan!'

'What's up?' asked the little old nurse.

'His Majesty the King is

up,' said the Butler. 'He's as up as a bottle of ginger-pop in hot weather.'

'On the rampage again, is he?' said old Nan.

'Rampaging something outrageous.'

'Ah,' nodded Nan, 'one of his fault-finding days.'

'One of his very worst. He's been down in the cellars finding fault with the cider-casks, the beer-barrels, the red wine, the white wine, the gooseberry wine, and me. And nothing wrong with any of us, Mrs Nan. I shall leave this day month.'

Before old Nan could remark on this, in waddled Cookie, the Cook.

'Mrs Nan! Mrs Nan!' she puffed.

'What's the matter?' asked the little old nurse.

'His Majesty's the matter.'

'Nollekens again! Poking in the kitchen, is he?'

'Poking is the word for it. He's poked his nose in the flour-bin, the sugar-bags, the salt-cellars, the pepper-pots, the jam-jars, the dripping-tub, and the

oven itself. Everything's wrong for him, though all's
as right as rain. I shall leave this day month.'

Next, in flew Megs the Dairymaid, wailing, 'Mrs
Nan! Mrs Nan!'

'What's *your* kettle of fish?' asked the little old
nurse.

'The King's my kettle of fish.'

'Meddling in the dairy, was he?'

'Meddling!' Megs threw up her hands. 'He mixed
the milk, kicked the cream-pans, battered the butter-
tubs, squeezed the cheeses, and whisked the whey
back into the curds just when I'd got 'em sorted out.
I won't stand such goings-on, that I won't. I leave
this day month.'

The bangings downstairs were now positively
deafening. Into the linen-closet stalked Jack the
Gardener. He was a stolid man, not given to speeches,
and he stood and stared before him till old Nan said
impatiently, 'Well, out with it!'

'Dandelions,' said the Gardener.

'Dandelions?'

'I said dandelions.'

'I heard you say dandelions.'

'Very well then,' said the Gardener. 'Dandelions
I said and dandelions you heard. And dandelions is
what I'm to grow in my flower-beds from this day
forth.'

'Who says so?' asked Nan.

'Nollekens,' said the Gardener.

'His Majesty the King?' asked Nan sharply.

'Nollekens,' repeated the Gardener.

'I'll thank you to speak of His Majesty respectfully.'

'*You* call him Nollekens,' said the Gardener.

'I'm his nurse. I've seen him in his bath.'

'Bath or no bath,' broke in the Butler, 'I won't have him shake up my wine-bottles.'

'He shan't poke his nose in my condiments,' puffed the Cook.

'He shan't meddle with my cream-pans,' vowed the Dairymaid.

'He shan't say what I grow in my flower-beds,' growled the Gardener.

And all four cried in one breath, 'We leave this day month!'

'Take thirty-one days' notice!' shouted a furious voice from the door, and there stood Nollekens himself, his face red with rage. He pointed his finger in turn at the Butler, the Cook, the Dairymaid, and the Gardener. '*Your* wine-bottles! *Your* condiments! *Your* cream-pans! *Your* flower-beds! I shall do what I like with *my* bottles, *my* condiments, *my* cream-pans, *my* flower-beds!' And the King banged about like a child in a temper.

'Stop it!' cried Nan from the top of the ladder. 'Stop it, I say, or I'll get down and spank you.' Noll stopped banging, and looked at her crossly, kicking his right-foot heel with his left-foot toe. 'Go straight into that corner,' commanded Nan, 'till I tell you to come out.'

31

Nollekens shuffled to the corner and stood there with his face to the wall.

'And you go back to your chores,' the nurse ordered John and Cookie and Megs and Jack.

'Yes, Mrs Nan,' they said meekly; and went.

Old Nan beckoned to young Jen, who had stood shaking in her shoes during this angry scene. 'Come you here and get what you asked for. Hold up your arms, child, I'm not made of elastic.' She counted the articles as she hung them over the between-maid's arms. 'Pair o' sheets. Ditto pillow-slips. Tablecloth. Ditto napkin. Bath towel. Face towel. Razor ditto. At *his* age!' sniffed old Nan. For though he was one-and-twenty, Nollekens would always be a little boy to

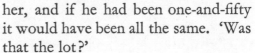

her, and if he had been one-and-fifty it would have been all the same. 'Was that the lot?'

'Pocket-hanky, please,' whispered young Jen.

'Ah,' said old Nan, 'we've a use for that here. Get along, and don't be all time about it.'

Young Jen got along in no time, and old Nan fetched out a fresh linen handkerchief smelling of lavender. 'Come here,' she commanded Nollekens, not unkindly.

He came, hanging his head, and stood by the ladder, where his chin came level with the old woman's shoulder.

'Wipe eyes,' said Nan,
dabbing the tears away.
'Blow nose.'

Nollekens blew hard
into the handkerchief.

'Going to be a good
boy now?' asked Nan.

'Yes, Nanny,' sniffed
Nollekens.

'Very well then.' Old Nan sat down on the ladder-
top and wagged her finger at him. 'What you want
to go being such a bad boy for?'

'How can I help it, Nanny? It's one of my bad
days. You know how it is,' explained Nollekens.
'Some days I'm just good and some days I'm just bad.
I've got a double nature, haven't I?'

'So's everybody,' said old Nan.

'Not so double as mine,' said Nollekens quickly.
'When I am good I am *very* very good.'

'When you are bad——' began his nurse.

'Yes, I'm horrid. I know. But Nanny, things do
up*set* me so.'

'That's no reason for upsetting things,' said Nan.

'Isn't it though!'

'What upset you this morning?' asked Nan. 'Got
out of bed the wrong side?'

'Both sides of my bed are the wrong side,' complained Nollekens. '*And* the top. *And* the bottom.
The sheets are as full of holes as a sheet of postage-
stamps. Look at that!' He pulled out of his pouch

33

a fine linen sheet that crumpled into shreds as it came.

'And look at *that!*' said old Nan. She put her hand in the cupboard and shook out the sheet that was its very twin. 'And that!' she went on, showing him a tattered pillow-slip. 'And that, and that, and that!' She produced towels, cloths, and napkins all in the same state. 'You don't have to tell *me*,' said old Nan.

'But Nanny, they're a disgrace!' shouted the King.

'They're a scandal,' said his nurse.

'We must get some new ones this instant.'

'Tell me where. There's no more linen to be had in the land.'

'I shall tell the Gardener to grow flax instead of dandelions,' Nolly decided.

'Oh, there's flax and to spare,' said she. 'Flax, and flax, *and* flax. Lift me down.' Nollekens lifted the little old thing off the ladder, and she pulled open the door of a huge store-cupboard. 'There you are!'

Nollekens looked in, and saw that the cupboard was stuffed to repletion with bales of raw flax.

'Well then?' he exclaimed.

'Who's to spin it?' she asked.

'The girls,' said Nollekens.

'The girls forsooth!' scoffed Nan. 'Much you know about girls. The girls nowadays are all giddy gadabouts or idle good-for-naughts.'

'*You* spin it then,' suggested Nollekens. 'You used to be a topping spinster, Nanny.'

'*Used* to be,' said old Nan. All of a sudden her old

cheeks wrinkled and crinkled, and flopping down on
the heap of flax she began to cry. 'My spinning-days
are dead and gone,' she wept.

Nollekens simply couldn't bear to see women cry.
He picked up his little nurse, sat down on a chair,
and jigged her up and down on his knee. 'There-
there, Nanny, there-there!'

'Such a handful as you've been,' old Nan wept
jerkily. 'Such a handful as you *are*.'

'There-there,' jigged Nollekens. 'I'm a good boy
now.'

'Till the next time comes along. You'll be the death
of an old body like me, you will.'

'I'll never be a handful any more,' promised Nolly.

'You think you won't, but you will,' wept old Nan.

'What can be done about it, Nanny?'

'You ought to get married.'

'Ought I, Nanny?'

'You really did ought, and take yourself off my poor
old shoulders, Nolly.'

'There-there, Nanny, I will.' Nollekens was ready
to promise her anything if only she'd stop crying. She
did so very suddenly, and sat up on his knee exceed-
ingly spry.

'You will, will you? Go picking some giddy gad-
about, or an idle good-for-naught. I know you!'

'I'll pick the best spinster in Norfolk, Nanny,' said
Nollekens, 'all to please you.'

'She better *had* please me! But don't tell me! You'll
pick her to please yourself.'

King Nollekens pointed to the bundles of flax toppling out of the cupboard. 'I'll pick anyone who can spin that.'

Old Nan hopped off his knee in a trice. 'Come along,' cried she, 'come along!'

'What for, Nanny?'

'To find her, of course.'

'Do you mean my bride?'

'I mean the one girl in Norfolk,' said old Nan, 'who can spin that flax.'

CHAPTER VI

Mother Codling is Flummoxed

Queen of Norfolk Dumplings!
Queen of Norfolk Dumplings!

So sang the voices in Doll Codling's daydream. She had fallen into a heavier doze than usual, as you are apt to do when you feel particularly comfortable inside. Mother Codling, coming back with the yeast from the baker's, found Doll nodding by the hearth. Nobody else was in the kitchen, though it was close on dinner-time. Mother Codling put down her packet and asked,

'Have the boys come agen from the fields?'

'No, mawther, not yet,' said Doll.

'Has Poll come agen from the shore?'

'No, mawther, not yet.'

'Have the dumplings come agen in the oven?'

Doll roused herself to peek inside the oven door. 'No, mawther, not yet.'

'They should ha' done,' said Mother Codling, untying her bonnet strings. 'Give 'em another five minutes.' She began to collect the plates and knives for dinner. 'And how many skeins have ye spun, time I was gone?' asked she. 'None, I'll be bound.'

'That's right, mawther,' said placid Doll.

'That's wrong, that is,' grumbled her mother.

37

'Whoever d'ye think is going to wed a gurt idle lazy-bones like you?'

'I don't mind, mawther,' said Doll.

'I do mind, darter. Am I to bake and brew for you all my born days?'

She began to set the table for seven, three a side for her children and one at the top for herself.

Poll came in, rather breathless, carrying her grass-filled creel. 'Mawther, where's the bird-cage?' she asked.

'So there you be at last,' said her mother. 'Did Charlee give you some good flounders?' She looked inside the creel, and threw up her hands. 'Lawks-a-mussy! what have you got there? *That's* no flounder.' She stared at the shining bird lying still in the grass, with its broken wing bound up.

'No, mawther, just think, mawther,' Poll explained eagerly, 'that's the Silver Curlew, and once upon a time she was the Lady in the Moon, but she flew away to look for Norwich Tower, and a hideous horrible hateful Thing ran out of the Witching-Wood to get her, and so it would have done only Charlee frighted him off, and mended her wing, and gave her to me to take care of. I'm sorry about the flounders, mawther, but there wasn't room in the creel for them both, and there's thousands and thousands of flounders but only one Silver Curlew in the world. Where's the bird-cage?'

And she ran to unhook a wicker cage from the wall. 'Thousands and thousands of flounders there may

38

be in the sea,' said Mother Codling, 'but if there's none in the creel I go hungry for my dinner.'

'I'll give you one of my dumplings,' said Poll, putting the sea-grass in the bottom of the cage.

'Which I can't abide or abear, as well you know,' said her mother. 'And look!' She pointed through the kitchen door. 'Here come the boys across the corn, famished as farmers. Haven't them dumplings come agen *yet*, Doll?'

Doll peeked again in the oven. 'Not yet, mawther.'

'That's a funny thing,' said Mother Codling. 'Give 'em another five minutes. Here you!' she raised her voice to call her sons. 'Abe! Sid! Dave! Hal! Stir your stumps, lads.'

Mrs. Codling's four boys came through the door in single file. Abe, who was tall, came first, Sid, who was small, came next, Dave, who was fat, came third, and Hal, who was lean, came last. But different as they were in shape and size, they all had one and the same thought in their heads.

'What's for dinner, mawther?'

'Dumplings,' said Mother Codling.

'Good!' said Abe, Sid, Dave, and Hal.

'Dumplings is grand,' said Abe.

'Dumplings is glorious,' said Sid.

'Dumplings is the best of food,' said Dave.

'Dumplings is *good*,' said Hal.

'There's Huffkins,' said Abe thoughtfully.

'And Biffens,' nodded Sid.

'And Baps,' Dave reminded them.

39

'There's Chitterlings and Chines,' said Hal.

'There's Pancakes, and Pikelets, and Parkins,' said Dave.

'There's Brandysnaps,' said Hal.

'Ah to be sure,' agreed the others, 'there's Brandysnaps.'

'But Dumplings is best,' said Abe. 'Dumplings is *good*.'

'Brawn!' said Sid.

'Bacon!' said Dave.

'Beastings!' said Hal.

'Barberry Jelly and Bilberry Jam,' said Abe.

'Furmenty!' cried Sid.

'Flummery!' cried Dave.

'Fraizes and Fadges!' cried Hal.

'*And* Fools,' said Abe.

'Sillabubs and Girdles,' said Sid.

'Cruddled Cream,' said Dave.

'Cakes!' said Hal. 'Fruity Cakes.'

'Doughy Cakes,' said Abe.

'Spongey Cakes and Spicey Cakes,' said Sid.

'Soda Cakes and Seedy Cakes,' said Dave.

'Cheeses!' squeaked Hal.

'Ah, Cheeses,' nodded the others.
'Cream Cheeses, Green Cheeses, Blue
Cheeses, Cheddars, and Cheshires.'

'Turmuts is scrumptuous,' said Abe.

'Trotters is sumptuous,' said Sid.

'Tripe is galumptuous,' said Dave.

'But Dumplings,' squeaked Hal,
'Dumplings is best of every food.
Dumplings is GOOD.'

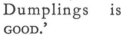

'Ah!' agreed
the others.

Then all four
yokels undid their
belts, sat down in their places at
the table, thumped on it with their
knives and forks, and shouted,
'Dinner!'

'Now then, Doll,' said Mother
Codling, 'your brothers are raven-
ing like crows in a beanfield. Fetch
out them dumplings.'

'I can't, mawther.

'What for can't you?'

'They ain't come agen yet.'

'Not none of 'em?' exclaimed Mother Codling.

'Not one of 'em,' said Doll.

'Dinner! dinner! dinner! dinner!' thumped the four
yokels.

41

'Come agen or not come agen,' said Mother Codling, 'we'll wait no longer. Fetch 'em out, and we'll eat 'em as they are.'

'But how can you,' asked Doll, 'if they ain't come?'

'What's the girl talking about?' cried Mother Codling, in an exasperated tone of voice. She came to look over Doll's shoulder into the oven, and once again she threw up her hands. 'Lawks-a-mussy!' gasped she, 'where 've they been and gone and got to?'

'Dinner! dinner! dinner! dinner!' thumped the yokels.

Mother Codling took Doll by the shoulders and shook her. '*What's—happened—to the—dumplings?*' she demanded.

'I've ate 'em,' said Doll.

'You've—ATE 'em?' repeated her mother.

'Yes, mawther.'

'All the lot of 'em?'

'Yes, mawther.'

'The *round dozen?*'

'Yes, mawther.'

Mother Codling paused to get her breath. Then she said heavily, 'You mean to tell me you've eat a whole bellyful of gurt big puffy duffy dumplings, *and you haven't got a bellyache?*'

'No, mawther.'

'Then you ought to have,' said Mother Codling. 'Shame on you!' cried she. 'Taking the very dumplings out of your starving brothers' mouths.'

'Shame on her!' groaned Abe.

42

'Shame! Shame! Shame!' groaned Sid, Dave, and Hal.

'I can't think what you're all making such a fuss about, I'm sure,' said Doll. 'What harm have I done, if I did eat 'em? Didn't you say,' she asked her mother, 'the dumplings would come agen in half an hour?'

'I'm flummoxed,' said Mother Codling. She collapsed on to a chair.

'My darter!' she ejaculated. 'Twelve dumplings. My darter ha' eat twelve dumplings. A dozen of dumplings my darter eat. In half an hour, she did, right off without stopping. All twelve of 'em. Twice six of 'em. Thrice four of 'em. I'm flummoxed. The whole round dozen in half an hour my darter did, the whole round dozen, she did.'

'The whole round dozen of what?' asked a voice in the doorway. And there stood a tall young man with a little old woman perched on his shoulder.

'Visitors, mawther,' cried Poll, jumping up.

The young man stooped his head, because of the little woman, and came into the kitchen, repeating his question. 'What was it your daughter did to flummox you so? The whole round dozen of what?'

Mother Codling stared him up and down, from the gold crown on his head to the gold buckles on his shoes. The next moment she was on her feet dropping curtseys.

'God bless us if it isn't the King of Norfolk! Get on your hindlegs, you louts,' she ordered her sons, 'and do deference.'

43

Abe, Sid, Dave, and Hal rose up from the table, pulled their forelocks, and sat down again.

'We are obliged,' said Nollekens. He set the little old woman down on the floor, and introduced her. 'My nurse, Mrs Nan.'

Mother Codling ducked, and introduced her younger daughter, who was staring at Nollekens with eyes as round as saucers. 'My little wench Poll,' she said.

'And a very nice little wench too,' said the King.

Poll bobbed, and Mother Codling said, 'We are obliged.'

Then Nollekens said for the third time, 'A round dozen of *what*? What were you saying just now? Why were you flummoxed?'

Mother Codling's face grew purple with embarrassment. She clutched at Poll and muttered, 'What'll I do?'

'Just tell him, mawther,' whispered Poll.

'Tell the shameful facts to the King and mortify the name of Codling? Never! Twelve of 'em,' said Mother Codling, her voice rising in spite of herself. 'Twelve of 'em, Poll!'

'Once and for all, twelve of WHAT?' demanded Nollekens frowning, for he couldn't bear to be kept waiting.

Poll stepped forward and said brightly, 'Twelve skeins of flax, sir.'

Mother Codling stared at her open-mouthed, but Poll only smiled and deftly twirled the spinning-wheel. 'The whole round dozen of skeins spun in half an hour. That's what flummoxed my mawther, if you please, sir. *And I hope he's satisfied now,*' she said to herself.

Whether he was or not she had no time to learn; for as soon as Poll had spoken, little Mrs Nan darted forward in a high state of excitement. 'Twelve skeins of flax in half an hour!' cried she. 'I never heard the like. No wonder you're all of a flummox,' she said to Mrs Codling. 'And your own child did it?'

'Yes, ma'am,' said Mother Codling faintly. 'My very own child as ever was.'

Nan turned her sharp eyes on Poll and pointed her finger. 'There stands your bride,' she said to Nollekens.

Nollekens looked anxiously from Poll to his nurse. 'But Nanny, she's too little.'

'She'll lengthen,' said Nan. 'Come you here, child.' Poll came obediently and stood in front of her. 'How old are you?' asked Nan.

'Twelve, if you please, ma'am.'

Once more the King protested, 'But Nanny, she's too young.'

'She'll olden,' said Nan. 'If a child of twelve years can spin twelve skeins in half an hour, what'll she do when she's twenty?'

'If you please, ma'am,' said Poll, 'it wasn't me that flummoxed my mawther.'

'Who was it then?' asked Nan.

'My sister there.'

She pointed towards the hearth; Nan and Nollekens turned and saw, for the first time, Doll looking placidly into the fire.

'Your sister?' said Nollekens to Poll.

'Your daughter?' said Nan to Mother Codling.

'Get up, you gurt gowk,' said the Miller's widow, 'and do deference.'

Doll rose slowly from her seat, bobbed to the King, and stood looking at him with her sweet lazy smile.

'She's comely,' said Nollekens to Nan, and then addressed the girl. 'It was *you* who did the round dozen?'

'Yes, please, your Majesty,' bobbed Doll.

'She's *very* comely,' said Nollekens to Nan.

'Beauty is but skin deep,' remarked his nurse. 'Come you here, young woman.'

Doll came and stood before Mrs Nan as Poll had done.

'How old may *you* be?' asked Nan.

'Eighteen come Michaelmas,' answered Doll, in her soft cooing voice.

Nollekens said, 'She's very, *very* comely, Nanny dear.'

'Tch, tch!' Nan pushed him aside. 'Are you a *good* girl?' she asked Doll.

'Yes, if you please, ma'am.'

'Have you got a sweetheart?'

'No, if you please, ma'am.'

'Oh Nanny!' cried Nollekens, 'she's most uncommonly comely!'

'Tch, tch!' snapped Nan again, and continued her questions. 'Young woman! did you really do what flummoxed your mother there?'

'Yes, if you please, ma'am. What I did flummoxed my mawther. I'm terrible sorry, ma'am, I couldn't help it.'

'Couldn't help it!' screeched Nan. 'You couldn't *help* spinning twelve skeins of flax in half an hour? *You couldn't help*——*!*' She broke off, at a loss for

47

words. Pointing at Doll, she said to Nollekens, 'There stands your bride.'

'The King's bride! Our Doll!' exclaimed Mother Codling.

'Well, did you ever?' said Abe.

'No,' said Sid, 'I never did.'

'Nor me,' said Dave.

'Nor me,' said Hal.

'What didn't you ever?' asked Poll, but they couldn't tell her.

While they were chewing their astonishment, Nollekens took Doll's soft plump hand in his.

'What is your name?' he asked.

'Doll, if you please, sir. What's yours?'

'Noll,' said the King. 'Would you like to be the Queen of Norfolk, Doll?'

'I'd like very well to be the Queen of Norfolk Dumplings,' said she.

'So you shall be, Doll, so you shall be, if——' The King squeezed her hand. 'If these pretty fingers can do what your mother says they can.'

Before Doll could answer, Mother Codling broke in quickly. 'Oh yes, sir, they can, that they can, I do assure you. Lawks-a-mussy!' she exclaimed with sparkling eyes, 'My Doll the Queen of Norfolk! The gentry kowtowing and bowing to my Doll!' She was

49

giddy for joy, and had to lean on the table. 'Is it all true, sir?'

Nollekens nodded. 'Look you here, mawther, I want a wife and I am going to marry your daughter. And look you here again. Three hundred and sixty-four days in the year she shall have all the vittles she likes to eat, all the gowns she likes to wear, and all the friends she likes to have about her.'

'Dumplings?' asked Doll.

'Dumplings by the galore, Doll.'

'A fancy gown of silk for Sundays?' asked Mother Codling.

'A gown of silk for every day in the week, mawther.'

'And can we come to Court too?' asked Poll eagerly. 'Can she have us about her? We're her friends, you know, as well as her family.'

'By all means, Poll,' smiled Nollekens. 'You can be about her for eleven months and thirty days of the year. But look you here again!' said the King, with a change of voice. 'On the thirty-first day of the twelfth month, Doll shall be shut in with a roomful of flax, and she shall spin it into thread for my sheets and my towels and my pocket-handkerchiefs.'

'Oh!' said Mother Codling. And 'Oh!' said her four sons.

'And if she don't,' went on Nollekens, 'I shall chop off her head.'

'*Oh!*' said Mother Codling. And '*Oh!*' said her four sons.

'I wouldn't like that,' said Doll.

'Of course you wouldn't, Doll,' agreed Nollekens, 'and so wouldn't I. I like you best with your head.'

Doll thought for a moment. 'Then what would you want to go and chop it off for?' she asked.

'Because I have a double nature,' said Nollekens. 'Haven't I, Nanny?'

'He has,' said old Nan to Mother Codling.

'On my bad days,' explained Nollekens, 'I get most *frightfully* cross. Don't I, Nanny?'

'He does,' said old Nan to Mother Codling.

'And then there's no telling *what* I'll be up to,' said Nollekens. 'Is there, Nanny?'

'There is *not*,' said old Nan to Mother Codling.

'So that's how it is,' said Nollekens. 'I can't help it, Doll, any more than you can help spinning. Well, there's no time like the present, is there?'

'So far as I can see,' said Doll, 'there's no other time at all.'

'I'm glad you agree,' beamed Nollekens. 'There *was* a time like yesterday, and there *will* be a time like tomorrow; but there *is* no time like today. So we'll prove it on the spot.'

'Prove what?' asked Poll.

'Whether Doll and your mawther are speaking the truth,' said Nollekens.

He clapped his hands very loud, and the open door was immediately darkened by a crowd of people. Three huge farm-carts drew up, one after the other, piled as high with unspun flax as carts at harvest-home are heaped with corn. At a sign from the king his servants began to unload the flax and bring it into the kitchen, stacking it all round the walls, on the table and chairs and dresser, and wherever they could find a place for it; while Mother Codling and her family looked on with their eyes popping out of their heads.

'There, my darling Doll!' said Nollekens, rubbing his hands. 'There's a sight to rejoice your spinster's heart! Now we will shut you in with all this lovely flax, and come again in half an hour.'

Doll looked at the mountain of flax, at her wheel, at the clock, at her mother, and at Nollekens.

'You'll—come—agen—in—half—an—hour?' she repeated, in stupefied tones.

'To the very second,' said Nollekens, 'and if all this beautiful flax is spun into shining thread, we'll be straightway wed. And if it *isn't*——'

'Yes, if it *isn't*?' Poll broke in.

'Off goes her head,' smiled Nollekens.

'But sir—your Majesty!' cried Poll, catching his hand. 'Oh, if you please, King! It wasn't——'

Mother Codling dragged her back before she could say any more. 'Mum, child!' she muttered. 'D'you want *all* our heads to go?'

'What's the matter with the child?' asked old Nan.

'Nowt, nowt!' said Mother Codling hastily. 'She's only flummoxed at the thought of the grand life to come.'

'Out!' cried Nollekens to the servants. 'Take the wains round the corner and scour them clean, to cart the thread away.' The servants obeyed instantly. 'Out!' he cried to the four yokels, and out went Abe and Sid and Dave and Hal. 'Out, Nanny! Out, mawther! Out, Poll!'

One after the other they went through the door, and Doll's round blue eyes followed them despairingly.

The King was the last to go. He stopped at the door, pulled out the key, and turned and smiled at his bride. 'In half an hour I'll come again, my Doll,' he said tenderly. Then he too went out, and turned the key in the lock.

CHAPTER VII

The Spindle-Imp

THE kitchen was so full of flax that there was no
room for the daylight to creep in at the window.
The fire sent a flicker of glowing shadows over
the heaped-up bundles, and by this red light Doll
stared at the flax, at her wheel, and at her soft useless
hands. What could she do? The best spinster living
couldn't have spun all that flax in a month of Sundays;
and instead of being the best, she was the worst
spinster in Norfolk. One little half hour she had to
accomplish her task, and the clock on the wall was
ticking the seconds away.

'O! O! O!' moaned Doll. 'What'll I do to save my noddle? In half an hour he'll come agen, and I'll have nothing to show. Well, if I can't, I can't. I shan't so much as try. I may as well enjoy my last half-hour in idleness.'

But what enjoyment, even in idleness, could there be for poor lazy Doll? She leaned her head on her wheel and sobbed and sighed.

The fire on the hearth began to crackle and spit. Something popped out of it just at Doll's feet. Thinking it must be a live coal she stooped to stamp it out, and what should she see but a little black imp with a long pointed tail, peering up at her.

'What are yew cryin' for?' asked the Imp.

'What's that to you?' asked Doll.

'Niver yew mind,' said the Imp. 'Just tell me what yew are cryin' for.'

'That won't do me no good if I do,' said Doll.

'Yew doon't know that,' said the Imp, twirling his tail round and round.

'No, I don't,' said Doll, 'that's why I'm asking.'

'And *I'm* askin' *yew* what yew 're cryin' for,' said the Imp.

'Well,' said Doll, 'that won't do no harm if that don't do no good, so I may as well tell you. My mawther kneaded twelve dumplings for dinner and put 'em to bake in the oven.'

'I bet that said they'd come agen in half an hour,' chuckled the Imp, twirling his tail, 'I bet that said so.'

'That's just what she did say,' said Doll.

'I bet you eated the dumplings all up, I bet you did,' chuckled the Imp.

'That's just what I did do,' said Doll. 'So my mawther was all of a flummox, and who should come by but the King of Norfolk, and asked why.'

'He, he, he!' chuckled the Imp. 'I bet that didn't tell him it was because you'd eated twelve dumplings.'

'No, she didn't,' said Doll. 'She told him it was because I'd spun twelve skeins of flax.'

At this the little black Imp twirled more madly than ever. '*Yew* spin twelve skeins,' he sneered. 'Yew couldn't spin one. Yew hain't got spinnin' thumbs. Look at those!' He spread out his fingers and held up two broad black thumbs under Doll's eyes. '*Them's* spinnin' thumbs,' he said conceitedly.

'What!' cried Doll. 'Can you spin?'

'Can I not!' said the Imp, strutting up and down.

'You see all that flax,' said Doll.

'Do I not!'

'You could never spin *that*.'

'Could I not!'

'Not in half an hour you couldn't,' said Doll.

'All the lot,' sneered the Imp, 'and twice as much agin.' And he puffed out his chest with conceitedness till it seemed fit to burst. 'I'm the Spindle-Imp, I am.' He twirled so fast that Doll almost lost sight of him.

'Stop it,' she said. 'If that flax is spun in half an hour I shall be the Queen of Norfolk.'

'And if that hain't?'

'If it isn't,' said Doll, 'I shall lose my noddle.'

'That'd be a pity, Doll Codling,' said the Imp. 'That's a pretty little noddle, that is. Dew yew want to lose yar pretty noddle, Doll?'

'No I don't then.'

'I'll tell yew what I'll dew,' said the Imp. 'I'll strike a bargain with yew. I'll spin yar flax for yew, Doll.'

'In half an hour?' cried Doll, clasping her hands.

'In next to no time,' said the Imp. 'But I'll want my pay.'

'I've only got fourpence now,' said Doll, 'but when I'm Queen I expect I'll have a bit more.'

'I can wait,' said the Imp.

'How long for?' asked Doll.

'A year from this day,' said the Imp.

'How much must I pay then?' asked Doll.

'P'raps nothing. P'raps a lot,' said the Imp.

'Well, let's hear it, whatever-you-call-yourself,' said Doll.

At this the Imp twirled like a teetotum. 'Whativer-I-call-mcself! He, he, he! Yew doon't know what I call meself, dew yew, Doll Codling?'

'I shall when you tell me,' said Doll.

'But I shalln't tell you, Doll, I shalln't *niver* tell yew my name,' he chuckled. 'A year from this day I shall come agen, and then yew must guess it. Nine guesses at my name is what I'll give yew. If yew dew guess it yew shall see me niver no more.'

'And if I don't?' asked Doll.

'If yew doon't guess my name, yew shall be mine.'

'I wouldn't like that,' said Doll.

'I would,' said the Imp. 'I would like it very much. That's the bargain, Doll Codling, that's my pay for spinning yar flax for yew.'

'Nine guesses?' said Doll.

'No more and no less. If yew fail in nine yew're mine! mine! mine!' And the Spindle-Imp stood on his head and twirled wrong end up.

'Stand up do, you're making me giddy,' said Doll.

The Imp stopped as suddenly as he had started, righted himself, and stared up at her with his eyes like hot coals. 'Is it a bargain, Doll Codling?'

'Well then it's a bargain,' agreed Doll. 'It's better than lose my noddle. A year's a long time, and nine's a lot of guesses. I reckon there can't be much more than nine names all told. I reckon I'll guess yours in one of them.'

'I reckon you woon't,' sneered the Imp. 'I reckon yew woon't, yew woon't, yew woon't! And then yew'll be mine, mine, mine!' And he puffed and he strutted and twirled his long tail.

'Get on with it do, you nasty little object,' said Doll. 'Time's running out.'

'Time's nothing to me,' said the Imp. 'Jest yew shut yar eyes and goo to sleep. That is, if yew can.'

58

'I always can,' yawned Doll, and went to sleep on the spot.

She couldn't have said if she had slept a minute or a year, but all through her slumber went a humming like millions of turning wheels, and the colour of her dream was as blue as flax-flower, and the smell of it was like linen fresh from the laundry. The humming stopped and she woke with a start and began to rub her eyes. The daylight was streaming in through the window, and the open door was thronged with people uttering cries of surprise.

'She's done it!' screamed Poll.

'She's done it!' gasped Mother Codling.

'She's done it!' grunted Abe and Sid and Dave and Hal.

'She's spun it!' exclaimed old Nan.

Then Nollekens strode into the kitchen and beamed down on Doll, who was stretching her arms and yawning. 'You've done it!' he said.

Doll looked round, as surprised as the rest of them. The huge bundles of flax had disappeared, and in their place lay beautifully spun hanks of fine yarn, all ready to be woven into linen. Well there! so the nasty little Spindle-Imp was as good as his word, thought Doll. She smiled dreamily up at Nollekens with her flax-blue eyes.

'Did I do it?' she said.

'*How* did you do it?' asked Nollekens.

'Ask me another,' said she.

'Well then I will,' said he. 'Will you marry me, Doll?'

'Well then I will, Noll,' said she.

'To church, to church!' cried old Nan. She had been examining the hanks of thread for flaws, and could find none. And had they not actually found Doll enjoying forty winks after accomplishing this astonishing feat in less than half an hour? Mrs Nan saw no point in delaying the royal wedding which would ensure the best spinster on earth as the King's bride; so, 'To church, to church!' cried she.

In another hour all Norfolk was loud with wedding-bells.

CHAPTER VIII

Poll comes to Court

WHEN the wedding had been celebrated and Doll became Queen of Norfolk, Mother Codling turned her mill over to the baker and followed her daughter to Court. Poll followed her mother, and Abe, Sid, Dave, and Hal followed Poll. For a month or so they hung about the Royal Palace, and tried to settle down.

But pretty soon Mother Codling missed her kitchen, for there wasn't room for two round Cookie's oven; and Abe and Sid and Dave and Hal missed their turmut-hoeing. So all five went back to the windmill, which was only a few miles along the coast, and instead of staying for life in the Royal Palace, they bundled themselves once a week into the blue waggon with red wheels, and came for Sunday dinner. In winter they had beef and Yorkshire and roast potatoes and cabbage and apple pie and cheese. In summer they had lamb and mint sauce and new potatoes and green peas and cherry tart and cream. At Michaelmas they had roast goose and plum pudding, and at Christmas they had crown of pork and mince pies. Having eaten well and snoozed it off, they bundled back into the blue-and-red waggon drawn by grey Dobbin, who was used to carting sacks of flour on weekdays; and with Mother Codling and the four yokels full of dinner in the cart he didn't know the difference.

But Poll stayed behind, and settled down with Doll in the palace for good. Both were as happy as the day was long. Doll had nothing to do but be waited on by a hundred servants. There was one to brush her hair, and another to lace her shoes, and a third to sew on her buttons, and a fourth to sugar her porridge. And there were ninety-six more to save her the trouble of doing the ninety-six other things we all do every day of our lives. In short, Doll had not to lift a finger for herself, which suited her down to a T. And she was so pleasant-mannered, and so pleasing to look at, and so pleased with everything and everybody, that it was a pleasure to serve her. Every morning when it was time to order the meals and Doll couldn't think of anything but dumplings, it was Cookie who made the suggestions and settled it all. Every morning Jack the Gardener sent in an armful of the best flowers for her room, and young Jen filled the bowls with water and arranged them. Every morning at eleven o'clock John the butler came up from his cellar with a glass of sherry wine, and Doll ran in from her dairy with a mug of rich milk, and, not to hurt their feelings, Doll drank them both. And every morning old Nan looked out fresh sheets for her bed and fresh towels for her rail; for since the wonderful spinning of the flax the linen-closet was now well stocked again.

As for Nollekens, he was twice as easy to get on with as when he was a bachelor; or rather, he was only half as difficult. He was devoted to his bride, who never set him on edge, and the batter-and-clatter in the palace had practically stopped. True, he had a little dust-up with Poll now and then, when they disagreed about something and started contradicting and calling names. But old Nan kept a sharp eye on them, punished them when she thought it was good for them, and made them ask each other's pardons before the sun went down. At heart they rather liked each other really, in spite of an occasional squabble; and Nollekens showed his better side by indulging Doll and Poll in their every whim. Doll had silk gowns and soft pillows to her heart's content; and when Nollekens asked Poll what she would like most, she asked for a very big bird-cage that she could get right inside while she tended the Silver Curlew. So Nollekens had one built in the garden where the sea-breeze could blow through it. It had three compartments: a bedroom filled with grass, round which a curtain could be drawn, a bath-room with a shallow tank full of sea-water, and a morning-room strewn with shingle, sand, and shells. Here Poll spent half her days, and sometimes half her nights, with the Silver Curlew, who fed from her hand and grew neither better nor worse. Poll went down daily to the shore, with a creel for fish, a pail for salt-water and seaweed, and a bag for silver sand to make the Curlew's cage a home from home. She was farther from Charlee's shack than she used to be, but some-times she chanced to meet him on the shore, and then she would ask him how long it would be before the

Curlew would be cured; but all he would say was, 'Time alone can tell.'

Poll loved her Curlew so dearly that she felt her heart would break when its wing was mended and she saw it fly away; but if the wing never mended she would be sorrier still. She had plenty besides to interest her in the palace. Cookie often let her stone raisins and stem currants in the warm kitchen, and Megs let her skim the cream off the pans in the cool dairy, and Jack let her pull up chickweed and bind-weed in the gay garden, and John would let her draw the King's supper-beer in the dim cellar. Moreover, they didn't seem to mind her asking questions about why you must beat batter in a draught, and which end of a blindworm was the blind one, and why you must never shake up a bottle of port (though you always must shake up a bottle of medicine), and why cream rose to the top if you left it alone. So Poll did not have much time to miss the mill, and if she suddenly longed to see Mother Codling and her brothers during the week, she could always saddle Noodles, the King's donkey, and ride there and back along the coast. On Sundays she saw them as regular as clockwork.

So the months passed very agreeably, and before the year was up the bells of Norfolk were set ringing again in honour of the birth of a baby princess. Nollekens ordered a salvo to be fired from a blunder-buss, but Nanny thought gunpowder was dangerous, so he popped his popgun three times instead from the top of the cliff. In a few weeks more the palace was as busy as a beehive with preparations for the Christening.

Cookie made and iced a huge cake full of currants and raisins and almonds and spice and rosewater. It had three tiers thick with sugar like drifted snow. The lowest and biggest tier was like a sugar flower-garden, the second tier was like a dovecot full of sugar doves, and the top tier was like a little temple with a baby's cradle inside it and a ring of sugar cupids dancing round it. When it was done the cake was seven foot high, and it took four able-bodied men to lift it. Abe and Sid and Dave and Hal were to have the honour of conveying it to the nursery. They had arrived the day before the Christening, so as to be in good time in the morning.

In the afternoon everybody was bustling about, draping new muslin curtains and tying them up with ribbons, and putting flowers everywhere, and polishing everything that could be polished, and carrying cans of hot water, and jugs of warm milk, and trays of powder and soap, and little downy pillows with lawn ruffles, and little fine vests and woolly shoes, and lacey veils and tissue paper—everything, in short, that goes with the christening of a baby princess. And Nollekens was getting in everybody's way, with his nose in an enormous book which he was reading from cover to cover.

He bumped into Poll on her way downstairs; she was going to the beach to get things for the Silver Curlew, but stopped to rub her elbow and say,

'Ow! What's that book?'

'It is a Book of Names,' said Nollekens. 'All the names ever thought of are printed in it, so the baby's name must be in here too, but I haven't found it yet.'

'Do you have to *find* it?' asked Poll.

'Of course.'

'Why can't you just *choose* it?'

'I might choose the wrong one. It is very important to give a baby its right name.'

'Is there only *one* right name?' asked Poll.

'Naturally. Don't be so stupid. Poll is *your* right name, isn't it?'

'Yes, but——'

'But what? Poll is your right name because you *are* Poll. You couldn't be Jemima if you tried.'

'If I'd been christened Jemima I shouldn't have to try,' said Poll, 'but I'm glad I'm not.'

'There you are then,' said Nollekens. 'If you can't be glad of your name it isn't the right one. I'll see that my baby is glad of *its* name when it grows up.'

'Then don't call it Jemima,' said Poll.

'You're not to tell me what I'm not to call it.'

'Why shouldn't I?'

'Because you've no say in the matter.'

'I'm its aunt, aren't I?'

'Aunts don't count,' said Nollekens.

'How do you know? You've never been one,' said Poll.

'I wouldn't be one if I could,' said Nollekens.

'You couldn't be one if you would,' retorted Poll.

'Don't answer backwards!' cried Nollekens.

'Stop squabbling, both of you,' commanded old Nan, coming by with a copper warming-pan full of hot coals, 'and get out of my way unless you want to be singed.'

Nolly flattened himself against the wall to make room for Nanny to pass, and Poll ran on down to the beach. There she found Charlee Loon, writing in the wet sand with a pointed stick.

'Hullo, Charlee,' she said.

'Hullo,' said Charlee.

'Well, hullo. What are you writing?'

'Can't say,' said Charlee. 'Water fills it up before I get there.'

'Why don't you write in the dry sand?'

'Then I'd have to make up my mind,' said Charlee, throwing his stick away. 'How's Silver?'

'She hopped twice yesterday and stretched her wing. Shall I take off the bandage and look?'

'Leave it to her,' said Charlee.

'I'm an aunt now,' said Poll.

'What of?'

'A baby. Can I have some fish?'

'For the thing you're an aunt of?'

'For the Silver Curlew.'

'Let her come for it.' Charlee stooped and curled his hand at the edge of the sea, where the next wave washed an opal shell into it. 'Give her this to remind her.'

'What of?' asked Poll.

'This or that, how should I know?' said Charlee. 'Some's reminded of one thing, some of another.'

'It's a lovely shell,' said Poll, stroking the gleaming whorls, and putting her eye to the twirly-whirly hole. 'I wish I could see inside. *Right* inside.'

'No good looking,' said Charlee. 'That's a listening shell. You get back home now, there's a sea-mist coming up.'

'There'll be a moon too, it's full moon tonight,' said Poll.

'Mist and moon, mist and moon,' said Charlee, and strolled away humming,

> *When I drew up my fishing-net*
> *What d'ye think was in it?*
> *A green-eyed sea-maid white and wet*
> *Singing sweet 's a linnet.*

Poll ran along the sand with the opal shell to her ear. Her footsteps filled with water as she ran.

CHAPTER IX

Naming the Baby

THE baby was being bathed when Poll got back.
It was the hour when everybody made some
excuse to pass through the nursery, where Doll
sat with a warm towel on her knees and the baby
cooing inside it. For this was a thing that Doll found
she wanted to do herself, and she did it as though she
had done it all her life. Her hands, that could not spin,
found that they could soap and dry and powder a baby,

slip its waving arms and legs into its tiny garments, and brush up the soft gold down on its head into a little shining quiff, as deftly as need be. Mother Codling and old Nan stood on either side telling her to do it *this* way, or advising her to do it *that* way, while Doll went on calmly doing it her own way, and tickled her baby till it smiled, and cuddled it till it drowsed. While she cuddled it, Doll crooned:

My white baby,
Smooth as a rose,
Smells so sweet
From her head to her toes,
Sweeter than beanfields and haycocks and clover,
I'll tumble and rumple and kiss her all over.

Which she proceeded to do just as Poll looked into the room before going along to see her Curlew.

'Been down to the shore then?' said Doll, glancing at the shell in Poll's hands.

'Yes,' said Poll, coming to her side and looking at the baby on Doll's knee. 'Hullo. I'm your aunt. Listen.' She put the shell to the baby's ear. 'That's the sea.'

'Take that dirty shell away at once,' said old Nan sharply.

'Sorry,' said Poll.

'Sea-salt's no dirt. Sea-salt never hurt anybody,' said Mother Codling.

'A shell straight off the shore is not the thing,' said old Nan stiffly. 'You don't know what's inside it.'

73

'The sea's inside it,' said Doll, 'to hush my baby to sleep. There, Poll, you can lay her in the cradle if you like.'

'Are your hands clean?' asked old Nan as Poll took the baby.

'Clean enough,' Mother Codling answered for her.

'Clean enough's not clean *enough* where a baby's concerned,' said old Nan.

'Pernicketty,' said Mother Codling.

Cookie came into the nursery with a bowl of gruel for Doll. She bent over the cradle to say, 'Pretty little dear.'

'Don't stand breathing there like a cow in a field,' said old Nan.

'A body must breathe,' said Cookie.

'Not over a new-born baby a body mustn't,' said old Nan.

'It shall have the most splendiferous christening cake in Norfolk, so it shall,' said Cookie.

'Is it iced yet?' asked Poll.

'All but the last cupid,' said Cookie.

'Can I come and do its wings?' asked Poll.

'And lick up the sugar droppings, I expect,' said Cookie good-naturedly. 'Come along then.'

As they went out Megs came in with a jug of cream for Doll's gruel. She stooped to chuck the baby under the chin.

'Tickle-ickle-ickle,' said Megs.

'Don't go poking the baby with your great finger,' said old Nan.

74

'La, Mrs. Nan, it likes a bit o' fun.'

'Not when it's digesting it doesn't,' said old Nan. 'Now what are *you* doing in here?' she asked the Butler, who had stalked into the room with a big book on a salver.

'His Majesty sent me,' said the Butler. He paused by the baby's cradle and said, with great dignity, 'Kutchykoo!'

'Don't go talking nonsense to the child,' said old Nan. 'It's got a brain like the rest of us.'

'Nonsense is sense to a baby,' said Mother Codling. 'Talk sense to it and you're talking nonsense. Diddle-iddle-ickums, then.' She leaned right over the cradle, breathing heavily, tickled the baby till it chuckled, and picked it up.

'Put it down,' said old Nan.

'I'm its granny,' said Mother Codling.

'I'm its nanny,' said old Nan.

Mother Codling glared at her. 'I always picked *my* babies up.'

Old Nan glared back. 'Nobody picks up *my* babies.'

'That don't go for grannies!'

'It always goes for nannies!'

The two old women ruffled at each other like a pair of angry hens.

'What a fuss about nothing,' said Doll. 'Give the baby to its mammy.'

She took the baby from her mother and kissed and cuddled it. Mother Codling nodded defiantly at old Nan, who merely said, 'Mammies have the right to the

75

last say.' But her voice bristled with disapproval. She turned her attention to the salver in the Butler's hands, and rapped the book with her knuckles.

'What did Nollekens want to send that in here for at this time of day?'

'His Majesty is coming to select the infant's nomenclature,' said the Butler.

'I'm going to call her Joan,' said Doll.

'Joan?' repeated Nollekens, appearing in the doorway.

'Yes.'

'Just Joan?' said Nollekens, coming into the room.

'Yes.'

'Why Joan?' asked Nollekens, sitting down by the cradle.

'I like it.'

'So do I,' said Poll, coming back from the kitchen, licking her sugary fingers.

Nollekens shook his head decidedly. 'Just Joan will never do. A single syllable! What will the Fairy Godmothers think of us?'

'Will there be Fairy Godmothers? Coo! how many?' asked Poll.

'I've invited four,' said Nollekens. 'If they accept, their godchild's cognomen must be worthy of them.'

'Who are they?' asked Poll.

'The Morning Fairy, the Noontide Fairy, the Twilight Fairy, and the Midnight Fairy. You could never call a child with four fairy godmothers merely Joan.'

'I don't see why not,' said Poll.

'What you don't see hasn't anything to do with it,' said Nollekens. 'What you don't see would make a fly laugh.'

'Why a fly?' asked Poll.

'Did you ever see a picture of a fly's eye?'

'No,' said Poll.

'If you had you'd know why.'

'I don't believe a fly *can* laugh,' said Poll.

'What you don't believe has nothing to do with it,' said Nollekens. 'What you don't believe would make a flea cry.'

Poll opened her mouth——

'And don't ask me why,' said Nollekens hastily, 'because I'm not going to tell you.'

'Don't you know?' said Poll.

'Never mind,' said Noll.

'Stop it,' said old Nan.

'Well,' said Poll, 'perhaps the Fairy Godmothers won't accept, and then Doll can call the baby merely Joan.'

'I'm going to call her Joan anyhow,' said Doll.

At that moment a carrier pigeon flew into the nursery, dropped four letters at Nolleken's feet, and flew out again.

'These must be the Godmothers' acceptances,' he said, opening the first letter, which was pink. 'From the Morning Fairy. She will preside with pleasure. Here's a gold envelope. From the Noontide Fairy. She's delighted to act.' Nollekens opened the third

letter, which was
blue. 'The Twilight
Fairy is charmed to
officiate.'

'The fourth one
is black,' said Poll.
'That's from the
Midnight Fairy.
She'll be there.'

'Is that all it says?' asked Poll.

'Yes, just she'll be there. So there
we are. Our baby will have her four
Fairy Godmothers. Not—*not* Joan,'
said Nollekens to Doll, speaking
very firmly.

'Joan,' whispered Doll to her
baby.

'What do *you* want to call it?' Poll asked Nollekens.

'Something polysyllabic,' said Nollekens, opening
the Book of Names. 'Four syllables at the mini*mum*,
one for each Godmother. Ha! here we are. Nicodemus.'

'Nicodemus is a boy's name,' said Mother Codling.

'And if it is?' said Nollekens.

'Our baby is a girl,' said Doll.

'Is it? Why didn't somebody tell me?'

'You've been told a dozen times,' said old Nan.

'Have I? Well, it's a pity. Nicodemus is a splendid
name. But I suppose it's too late to change it.'

'To change what?' asked Poll.

Naming the Baby

'The baby.'

'Well I should think so!' snorted old Nan. 'It's the name that must be changed.'

'The name isn't going to be changed,' said Doll. 'The name is Joan.'

CHAPTER X

Feathers and Flax

THE women bustled away with the bath-water and the damp towels, leaving Poll and Doll and Nollekens with the baby. Nollekens shut the Book of Names regretfully.

'Joan,' he repeated. 'I don't like Joan at all. Well, all I can say is, it's a pity. Come to daddy,' he said, taking the baby out of Doll's arms and examining it critically. 'I must say it's a credit to me. Hair as fair as flax and eyes as blue as flax-flower. And that reminds me,' he said, handing the baby back. 'The flax-harvest is simply super this year.'

'Is it?' yawned Doll.

'A record. There's good news for you!'

'Why?'

'Why? Have you forgotten what day it is today?'

'It's our wedding-day to be sure,' said Doll, 'a year gone by.'

'A year gone by. Precisely.'

Doll gave a little gasp.

'You *haven't* forgotten, I see,' said Nollekens gaily. 'Yes, my poppet, all the flax has been gathered and is being piled at this very moment in the next room. Twice as much as last year. Isn't that splendid! And today you must spin it or lose your lovely noddle.'

'But I'm the Queen now,' said Doll faintly.

'Queens must stick to their bargains like other women,' said Nollekens. 'Even more so.'

'But the Christening's tomorrow,' pleaded Doll.

'All the more reason to do the spinning today.'

'And suppose I don't,' said Doll slowly.

'Then we'd have to have the Christening without you,' said Nollekens, 'and that *would* be a pity.'

'Oh, you can't mean it, Nolly, indeed you can't. What have you got against me?' asked poor Doll.

'Me, Dolly? I've got nothing against you, nothing whatsoever. I'm prouder of you than if you were the Queen of Sheba. Aren't you the champion spinster in East Anglia?'

'And don't I wish I *was* a spinster again!' flashed Doll. 'Don't I wish I *was* the Queen of Sheba. Nobody expected *her* to twirl a spindle. I wish I was a lily in the field. *They* don't have to spin a record crop of flax. It's unfair—it's unreasonable, that's what it is! It's *unkind*.'

This put the King's dander up. 'Unkind? Unkind? Unkind?' he shouted. 'How dare you say I'm unkind? Unfair, yes! I am not fair. Unreasonable, I grant you! I've never been reasonable. But *unkind*? How can I be *un*kind when that's the kind I am?'

Poll jumped to her feet and ran at him full tilt. 'That's *one* of the kinds you are, you—you—double-natured brother-in-law, you!'

'So *you* must come butting in, must you?' bawled Nollekens, 'you—you feather-brained chit of a sister-in-law!'

'I'm *not* feather-brained,' cried Poll, stamping her foot at him.

'You *are* feather-brained,' cried Noll, stamping his foot at her. 'And no wonder, sitting over that silly bird of yours, morning, noon, and night. I've a good mind to have it banished.'

'Don't you touch my bird! Don't you dare touch my bird!' squealed Poll.

'I wouldn't touch your bird with a pair of filigree sugar-tongs.'

'You haven't got a pair of filigree sugar-tongs.'

'I shall have some made,' said Nollekens, 'especially not to touch your bird with. Nursing a sick curlew all the year round!'

'It's getting better,' Poll declared.

'It's not. It's getting worse, and *worse*, and WORSE. It'll pop off tomorrow, ha, ha!'

'It hopped yesterday, twice.'

'I don't believe it.'

'I *saw* it.'

'*I* didn't see it.'

'You weren't there.'

'Keeping it in a ridiculous cage as big as a rather small bathroom,' jeered Nollekens. 'Feathers on the brain, that's what's the matter with *you*.'

'That's better than flax,' retorted Poll. 'That's what you've got on *your* brain. Flax!'

'Feathers!' bawled Nollekens.

'Flax!' screamed Poll.

'Feathers, feathers, feathers!'

'Flax, flax, flax!'

And they stamped at each other, beside themselves
with temper.

The noise brought Mother Codling running in.

'Lawks-a-mussy! Don't you stamp at my little girl,'
she cried. 'You ought to know better than stamp at
a little girl like that, a great big king like you.'

But Nollekens only stamped again, harder than ever.

'Feathers!' cried he.

'Flax!' cried Poll.

'A great big king like you!' cried Mother Codling.

In waddled Cookie, with the salt-box in one hand
and the sugar-bowl in the other.

'Hold your row, can't you?' she said. 'I can hear you right down in the kitchen. How can a body think with this rumpus going on? You've made me mix the sugar with the salt.'

'Feathers!' cried Nollekens.

'Flax!' cried Poll.

'A great big king like you!' cried Mother Codling.

'I've been and mixed the sugar with the salt!' cried Cookie.

'What's going on?' inquired the Butler, appearing at the door.

'What's a-going on?' inquired the Gardener, looking through the window from the top of a ladder.

'He's got flax on the brain,' and 'She's got feathers on the brain,' cried Poll and Noll in one breath.

'A great big king like him!' expostulated Mother Codling.

'They've made me mix the sugar with the salt!' complained Cookie.

'Nice goings on!' said the Butler; and

'Nice a-goings on!' said the Gardener.

For the next two minutes nothing was heard but a hubbub of 'Flax!' 'Feathers!' 'A great big king like you!' 'The sugar's in the salt!' and 'Nice goings on!'

'SILENCE!'

Old Nan was in their midst, looking from one to another with severe disapprobation. The hubbub stopped instantly, and there was dead silence.

'Well?' said Nan.

Nobody answered.

She looked Nollekens up and down with her bright beady eyes. 'What have you got to say for yourself?'

Nollekens pointed sulkily at Poll. 'She stamped her foot at me.'

'Who stamped first?' cried Poll.

'You did,' said Nollekens.

'*You* did,' said Poll.

'Oh you story!' said Nollekens.

Poll tossed her head. 'P'raps I did then. But you called me a featherbrain.'

'So you are,' said Nollekens.

'I'm not,' said Poll.

'You *are*,' said Nollekens, and stamped his foot.

'I'm *not*,' said Poll, and stamped hers.

'You said I'd got a double nature,' whined Nollekens.

'So you have,' asserted Poll.

'YOU KNOW YOU HAVE!' cried everybody, before Nollekens could deny it.

Nollekens got very red. He ran to old Nan, whimpering, 'They're crossing me, Nanny, and when I'm crossed I'm cross.'

'Go straight to your room,' said old Nan in her sternest voice, 'pull down the blinds, stand in a corner, and count a-thousand-and-one.'

Nollekens shuffled to the door, hanging his head. When he got there he turned and made a face at Poll.

'Feathers!' he sneered.

'Flax!' jeered Poll.

Old Nan pounced on her. 'You too!' she commanded.

'You're no better than he is. A-thousand and-one, mind, the pair of you. *And no skipping.*'

She marched them out of the room. Mother Codling, Cookie, and the Butler faded after them, and the Gardener faded out of the window.

Doll was left alone in the nursery with her baby, who had slept like a lamb through it all.

CHAPTER XI

ℕine Guesses

'OH me, my baby!' sighed Doll. 'Oh me, what shall I do? Fair as the flax, blue as the flax-flower, and a record crop to spin. Whatever shall I do, oh me, oh me? I'll never live to see your Christening-day.'

And at the thought of the roomful of flax awaiting her, Doll fell from sighing to sobbing, with her face in her hands.

'What are yew cryin' for?' asked a voice at her elbow.

'None of your business,' sobbed Doll. Then she took her hands from her face, and uttered a little scream. 'I declare! if it isn't you!'

Beside her stood the little black Spindle-Imp, twirling his tail.

'Yis,' he sniggered, 'that's me. He, he, he! that's me, me, me!'

'What have you come for?' asked Doll.

'Hoo, hoo, hoo! for yew, yew, yew!' sniggered the Imp. 'The year is up, Doll Codling. Yar mine! yar mine!'

'Don't talk such nonsense,' said Doll.

'T'ain't nonsense, yar mine,' said the Imp.

'I'm nothing of the sort, Mister Whats-your-name.'

'Whats-me-name, whats-me-name,' chuckled the

Imp. 'That's what yew doon't know, Doll Codling, that's what yew'll niver know till I've got yew safe and sound whar nobody 'll niver set eyes on yew agin.' He began to caper about with horrid glee, and fetched up beside the cradle. 'What's this yew've got here, Doll Codling? So sure as I dew live that's a little baby.'

He poked with his black finger, but Doll quickly snatched the baby up out of his reach.

'Leave it be, you nasty sooty imp! Leave my baby be,' she cried, cuddling it close.

'Yar fond o' yar baby, are yew?' said the Imp.

'That I am.'

'Yew'd be sorry to leave that,' said the Imp.

'That I would. But I'm never going to leave you, am I, my precious?' crooned Doll.

'Hain't yew, Queen Doll? We'll see about that,' said the Imp. 'If yew doon't guess my name in nine, this instant minute, yew'll leave yar baby for iver and a day.'

'You wouldn't have the heart!' cried Doll.

'No, I would *not* have the heart,' said the Imp, 'and for why? Becos I hain't got a heart, and yew can't not have what yew hain't not got. He, he, he! Guess me in nine or yar mine, mine, mine! Come now, what's my name?'

'That's Bill,' guessed Doll.

'Noo that hain't,' said the Imp. 'Thar goos one!' He twirled round and round with glee.

'That's Ned,' guessed Doll.

'Noo that hain't. Thar goos two.' And he twirled again, still faster.

88

'Is that Mark?'

'Noo that hain't. Thar goos three!'

'Then that's Sammle.'

'Noo that hain't. Thar goos four!'

'A-well, is that Methusalem?' guessed Doll.

'Tain't that norther. Thar goos five!'

'Then that must be Zebedee.'

'Tain't, 'tain't, 'tain't! Thar goos six!'

Doll began to feel anxious as she cudgelled her brains for another name.

'I reckon that's Hasdrubal,' she said.

'I reckon that hain't. Thar goos seven!'

Now Doll was fairly frightened, for she had only two guesses left. In a shaking voice she said,

'Certain-sure that must be Nebuchadnezzar.'

'Tain't, 'tain't, 'tain't. Thar goos eight!' chortled the Imp. 'One more, Doll Codling, yew've only one more guess.'

What should Doll say? Were there any more names in the world? She felt too dazed to think. As she looked about her in despair, her eyes lit on the big Book of Names which Nolly had left on the salver.

'*I* know your name,' she cried triumphantly.

'Noo yew doon't, noo yew doon't,' jibed the Imp.

'I do, I do, I do! That's Nicodemus.'

At this the Imp chuckled,

> *He, he, he!*
> *Thar goos nine!*
> *Come along o' me,*
> *Yar mine, mine, mine!*

Then he twirled right round the room, and fetched up again beside the cradle.

'Say farewell to yar mammy, little baby. A pretty little baby, tew be sure. Say farewell to yar little baby, Doll.'

'No, no, no, no, no!' cried Doll.

The Imp reached out his little black hand, but before he had touched her his eyes filled with cunning, and he said,

'A-well, tis a pity tew part a baby from its mammy. I'll tell yew what I'll dew. I'll let yew bring yar little baby with you.'

'Bring my baby to the horrid place you live in?' said Doll, shuddering.

''Tis a bewtiful place I live in,' snarled the Imp, 'a bewtiful place! And yar baby's a bewtiful baby tew live in it. I like yar baby as much as I like yew. I'll tell yew what I'll dew. I'll strike a bargain. I'll give yew another night tew think it over, and tomorrow when I come agin yew shall have three more guesses at me, and if yew doon't guess me *that* time, yew and yar baby shall come tew me for iver.'

'And if I do,' said Doll, 'you'll go away for ever?'

'That's a bargain, Doll Codling.'

Doll thought, and said, 'It's all or nothing then, and that's a bargain. But—oh me, oh me, oh me!' And she wrung her hands.

'What's yar trouble now?' asked the Imp.

'Flax is my trouble. Today I must spin the flax-crop before nightfall, or off goes my noddle.'

'A-well,' said the Imp, 'I woon't lose my bargain for a thimbleful of spinning. I'll spin yar flax for yew, Doll. But yew'd best come along o' me this instant minute.'

'That I won't then,' said Doll with spirit. 'I'll neither come with you nor lose my noddle. Three guesses you've promised me, and I'm certain sure I'll guess you in one of them.'

'Noo yew woon't,' said the Imp. 'Noo yew woon't. Nobody can't niver guess my name, in three times three and ninety times nine. I'll keep my promise and yew'll keep yours, Queen Doll. Today I'll spin yar flax, and tomorrow yew and yar baby shall be MINE.'

With that he twirled and he twirled and he twirled till Doll was obliged to rub her dizzy eyes. When she stopped rubbing, the Spindle-Imp was nowhere to be seen.

CHAPTER XII

Poll and Doll

'NINE-HUNDRED-AND-NINETY-SEVEN, nine-hundred-and-ninety-eight, nine-hundred-and-ninety-nine, One Thousand—and ONE,' gabbled Poll at the nursery door. 'There!' she said, coming in, 'I've beaten Nolly. He got muddled in the Seven Hundreds and had to begin again. Hullo! I'm your aunt,' she said, peering into the cradle, but the cradle was empty. 'Where's baby? Oh, you've got her. Can I?'

Doll was clasping the baby tightly in her arms. Poll reached up and took her. 'I think she's beginning to know me. I'm glad you're not crying any more.'

'It's gone past crying,' said Doll.

'What has?' asked Poll. 'What *were* you crying for? Was it because Nolly was a pig? Pooh, Nolly!' Doll shook her head. 'Then was it because you've got to spin flax today? But look at what you did last year! If you did it then you can do it now.'

'But I didn't,' said Doll.

'Wonderful! you were simply wonderful,' Poll ran on without attending. 'I couldn't believe it was you.'

'But it wasn't,' said Doll.

'Wasn't?'

'No.'

'Wasn't *you*?' repeated Poll, knitting her brows.

93

'What do you mean? We all of us saw that flax spun as fine as fine. If it wasn't you, who did?'

Doll did not answer, and something in her manner as she sat there made her little sister look at her attentively for the first time. Laying the baby back in its cradle, Poll knelt down and put both her arms round Doll's waist.

'Tell us,' coaxed Poll.

Still Doll seemed unable to speak, and now Poll grew alarmed.

'Don't frighten me, Doll,' she begged. 'Tell us. If you didn't do it, who did?'

'A nasty little sooty imp of mischief did it,' whispered Doll.

'A nasty little—— What *are* you talking about? Who *is* he?'

'If only I knew!' cried Doll. 'If only I knew!'

Poll took her by the shoulders and gave her a shake. '*Talk*,' she urged. 'Don't be mysterious. You've never been mysterious before. Talk, talk, talk!'

The words came tumbling out of Doll's mouth pell-mell, like dried peas pouring through a hole in a paper bag.

'I were shut in with my spinning-wheel and up pops this little black imp, and that twirls that's tail and bargains to spin the flax if I can guess his name come another twelve-month. And if I can't he'll come and make me his. So I think, a year's a long time, I think, so yes, I says. And today the twelve-month's up, and that little sooty twirling imp has come for me.'

94

'He's *come* for you?' repeated Poll, staring round the room. 'But you're still here, Doll.'

'He's come and gone. He'll come agen tomorrow. This time he wants my baby as well as me.'

'WHAT!' said Poll in the loudest voice she had.

'So he's to spin the flax again today,' moaned Doll, 'and if I don't guess him tomorrow he'll have us both.'

Poll took her arms away from Doll's waist, and threw them round the cradle instead. 'My *niece!* He'll have my niece? I'd like to see him!'

'You wouldn't,' said Doll. 'He's the worst thing to see I ever saw. Oh me, if only I knew his ugly name! Nine guesses I made, all wrong. Three guesses I'll make—and they'll be wrong too, they will. It's farewell to you all for my baby and me.'

'It's not!' Poll hugged the cradle tightly. 'It's not, it's not! I won't let it!'

'You can't stop it,' said Doll, 'if we don't find out his name.'

Poll sprang to her feet and clenched her fists. 'Then I'll find out his name. I *will*. I'll find out his name.'

'What name will you find out?' said old Nan, coming in with a pile of clean nappies. Doll gave Poll a warning look, but old Nan didn't seem to expect an answer. She thought they were still discussing the Christening, and her attention was diverted by Nollekens, who just then came to the door, counting carefully.

'Nine-hundred-and-ninety-eight, nine-hundred-and-ninety-nine, One-Thousand-precisely, One-Thousand-and-One. There, Nanny!'

Old Nan reached up and patted his cheek. 'Good boy now?'

'Yes, Nanny, good boy now,' said Nollekens, and, very pleased with himself, he repeated to Doll, 'I'm a *good* boy now. Oh!' he exclaimed with great concern, 'you've been crying. My Doll mustn't cry, you know, that won't do at all.' He pulled out his pocket-handkerchief and dabbed her cheeks. 'I can't bear my darling Doll to make her eyes red.'

Doll looked up hopefully. 'Can't you, Noll? Then do you mean I needn't spin the flax?'

'Was *that* why you were crying? But of course,' cried Nollekens merrily, '*of course* my darling Doll shall spin her flax. Just take a look at it!'

He unlocked a door that led into an adjoining room,

where Abe and Sid and Dave and Hal were stuffing flax ceiling-high, one bale on top of another.

'Pile it up, pile it up, boys!' cried Nollekens. 'Your sister's crying her eyes out for it.'

'Oh me,' sighed Doll.

But Nollekens was rubbing his hands and didn't hear her. He fussed round the four yokels, directing them here and there.

'Oh me, oh me,' sighed Doll, again and again.

Poll ran to her and whispered fiercely, 'Doll! *run away.*'

'Run?' said poor Doll. 'Run where?'

'Never mind where! Pick up our baby and run away. Run away from Nolly. Run away from that little black imp.'

'What's the good?' said Doll. 'That pops up all over the place. There's no saying where that'll pop up next.'

'He, he, he! he, he, he!' came a chuckle.

Poll looked round, startled, and saw a queer little black thing leering at her out of a bundle of flax in the next room. As swiftly as it had shown itself it vanished again.

'Was that That?' she whispered.

'That was That,' whispered Doll.

'He's horrid, horrid, horrid!' cried Poll angrily.

'Who's horrid, horrid, horrid?' asked Nollekens. 'You can't mean me, because I'm very nice just now.'

'I didn't mean you,' said Poll.

'Then I don't mind whom you meant,' beamed

97

Nollekens, 'and I'm not going to do any more quarrelling with anybody today. Up with you, Dollikins. The flax is all in, so in you go too.'

'Must I, so soon?' said Doll, looking wistfully at the cradle.

'Sooner begun, sooner done,' said old Nan. 'I'll look after baby till you come again.' She picked the baby out of the cradle and rocked it in her arms. 'Didsums-idsums-iddy then! Time we went by-byes. There's the moon coming up. Who's Nanny's ickle oozie-woozie-woo?'

It was lucky that Mother Codling couldn't hear her.

CHAPTER XIII

The Silver Curlew

ALL was quiet in the palace.

Doll was locked in the room from which the faint whirr of spinning might have been heard through the keyhole, if anyone had cared to put an ear to it. But nobody did. Everyone took it for granted that what Doll had done last year she would do this.

The baby was asleep in old Nan's room, and one after another Mother Codling, Cookie, Megs, and young Jen had tiptoed in to peep at it before they too went to bed.

Nollekens was up in the garret, where he was laying out the rails and points and signals for his train. When he thought everybody was asleep he sneaked down to the coal-cellar to get some real coal for the coal-wagon, which Nanny would be sure to disapprove of; so he took off his shoes and crept in his stocking-feet. Before he came up again he passed the larder, which made him feel hungry very suddenly; so he looked in and helped himself to a slice of pie and a lump of cake. Then he began to creep up again; but on the way he passed his bedroom door, and the pillows looked so inviting that he thought he would lie down on them to eat his pie before he went back to his train. Half-way through the pie he fell asleep, and was soon snoring with his cheek on the lump of cake.

99

And everybody else all over the palace was either snoring or sleeping soundlessly.

Only Poll was awake. She had slipped out of the palace before her mother could order her to bed, just as she was about to begin her great adventure. But first she went to wish her curlew good night. It was preening its silver plumage, and did not pay her much attention, and she stepped out of the cage feeling rather lonely. The world seemed very big, and she felt very little, and she had not the least idea where the Spindle-Imp lived, or which way to turn to find him. Meanwhile he was spinning away for Doll's dear life in the flax-room; but he would not be there long. If last year he had accomplished the huge task in half an hour, this year he would do it in an hour at most. It was no use trying to tackle him face to face; he would sneer and jeer and fleer, and never let her trick his name out of him. Her best plan, thought Poll, was to find his home before he got back, hide near by, and hope to hear him addressed by those whom he lived with.

She could see the light in Doll's room from where she crouched by the bird-cage. He's still there, thought Poll; would it be better, after all, to wait awhile in the garden on the chance of seeing him leave the palace, and following? Yes, that was the best plan. So Poll crouched on, watching the moon rise, and the pale moths come out, and the white owl flit, and the stocks in the garden double their scent. Before she knew it she had fallen into a doze. When she opened her eyes the moon was high in the sky and the lights in the palace windows were out. Far away the bells in Cromer church tower were chiming midnight.

Oh you silly! thought Poll. You've missed your chance. He's gone, and what will you do now? She could have cried with vexation for her carelessness. Now she must start her adventure without any idea whether she should go north to Wells or south to Caister or west to Aylsham or east into the sea. Her knees felt stiff, and putting her hand down on the ground to help herself up she felt something in the grass. It was the opal shell which the sea had drifted that day into Charlee's palm. She put it to her ear, and heard the wash of the wind and the whisper of waves.

The wind goes everywhere, thought Poll, the wind knows everything. It goes all over the world and you can't stop it. You can keep out the sun and the rain, but you can't keep the wind out. It can go through cracks and keyholes and down chimneys. Wherever that black imp lives, the wind has been there one time or another. I wish I could speak the language of the wind. I wish it could answer questions. I wish my shell could speak in my ear what the wind is saying.

Swish-swash, murmured the shell, *wish-wash, swish-swash*.

Poll shut her eyes and began to whisper to the shell, hushing her voice to a sort of muzzy murmur, hoping it was a sound the shell would understand and answer.

Shell, shell,
murmuring shell,

tell, tell,
tell me the name,
tell in my ear
the name, the name,
tell, tell, tell
his name
who comes to claim
our dear, our dear,
shell, shell,
tell me his name.

Swish-swash, murmured the shell in her ear, *wish-wash, swish-swash.*

It was the same language as before, as vague and past human understanding.

Suddenly it was pierced by another sound. '*Me-uuu! me-uuu! mee-uuuu!*'

The birds are crying over the waves, thought Poll, the birds are crying through the wind.

'*Mee-uuuu!*'

But surely this sound did not issue from the shell? Surely Poll heard it through her open ear. She unclosed her eyes, which felt a little sticky from being so fast-shut. At first the moonlight made everything swimmy and she could only see a sliding silver movement over the grass that seemed to be the wind made visible. Then as her eyes cleared Poll caught and held her breath. What did she see? She saw the Silver Curlew floating above the flower-beds like a large moth. It rose a little, dipped, rose a little higher, and slid to earth again. Poll watched its movements

anxiously. It stepped through the dewy grass as though it were stepping through sea-weed, and stopped beside the fountain to wet its bill. Re-freshed, it began to try its wings again.

'You're better!' whispered Poll, half to herself, half to the Curlew. 'You're well! You can fly!'

For now the bird rose higher in the moonlight, and glided with its old grace along the wind. Some minutes passed while it pursued its delicate dance, half in air, half on earth, ascending higher in each flight, and descending to its foothold as its wings tired.

At last it seemed to have gained full confidence in its powers, and rose so high that Poll could only see a silver spark in the sky. She reached out her hands, crying to it——

'Don't go, don't go! Show me the way, Silver Curlew, show me the way!'

The next moment the bird swooped down like a shooting-star, and Poll could not tell whether she had shrunk to the size of a mouse or the Curlew had swelled to the size of an angel. All she knew was that she became enveloped in a cloud of moonshine, and was wafted away like a tuft of gossamer.

CHAPTER XIV

Lost in Memory

THE moonglade on the sea made a road from the
edge of the shore to the horizon. It was broad
where the shallow waves lapped the sand, and
tapered to a point where it touched the rim of the sky.
Charlee was done for the day. He had beached his
boat and supped his cold plum porridge, and pulled
his whistle out of his pocket. At the first notes the
three puffins came paddling about him, hopeful of a
tune to dance to. Charlee lay at ease on his back, and
set them off with a few stray notes; then he sat up
with his hair full of sand, and made a song for them.

Three little puffins
Were partial to muffins,
As partial as partial can be.
They wouldn't eat nuffin
But hot buttered muffin
For breakfast and dinner and tea.
Pantin' and puffin'
And chewin' and chuffin'
They just went on stuffin', dear me!
Till the three little puffins
Were chockful of muffins
And puffy as puffy can be,
All three
Were puffy as puffy can be.

The puffins puffed and pranced with solemn enjoyment, but whether they had really had muffins for tea is a very moot point.

Presently all three stopped as one puffin, their heads cocked on one side. Out of the air came a far-off cry of 'Char—lee! O—O! Chaar—lee!'

In the twink of an eye the puffins scuttled away. Charlee put his whistle in his pocket and stood up, gazing into the sky. In the distance appeared what seemed first to be a little wind-driven cloud; but no cloud ever sailed so swiftly across the moonlit dome as this one on silver-feathered wings that grew larger and larger, and soon glided down to the shore in the shape of a great bird with a little girl on its back.

'Hullo,' said Poll, slipping on to the sands. 'Coo! that was lovely. Hullo, Charlee.'

'Hullo,' said Charlee.

Poll looked round in puzzlement. Her wits were still spinning from her flight through the sky. Only a moment before she had been in the King's garden, and now here she was on the beach. 'What am I here for?' she asked.

'You tell me,' said Charlee.

'I can't,' said Poll. 'I don't know why. The Curlew brought me.'

'Ask her then,' said Charlee.

'She's well again,' said Poll.

'So I see.'

'And she's seven times as big as she was when she was ill.'

'Is she?' said Charlee.

Poll looked, and there was the Curlew, no bigger than another, dipping about the shore.

'Curlew,' said Poll, 'what did you bring me here for?'

The Curlew paid no heed.

'P'raps she hadn't any particular reason,' said Poll.

'Everything has a particular reason,' said Charlee.

'Have you?' asked Poll.

'Once I did, once I did.' He glanced sidelong at the Curlew. 'Want a fish?'

He offered the Curlew a herring from his catch. She took it daintily in her beak and tossed it away.

''Tweren't that then,' said Charlee. 'What did you bring Pollee here for, Silver?'

The bird paid him no more heed than she had Poll. Her dipping movements turned into a dance. She seemed to weave it like a silver thread, and suddenly she hunched her feathers into a squat shape, and twirled round and round.

'She's spinning, look,' whispered Poll. 'And now, oh look! She's shrunk herself into a dwarf like—like who?'

The Curlew rose a little above the sand, and her shadow hopped there grotesquely as she moved. Poll clutched Charlee's arm.

'Curlew! Curlew! who is it you're like?' she cried.

'I know,' muttered Charlee hoarsely, '*I* know who she's like. She's taken the shape of the worst thing in the Witching-Wood.'

'Do you mean a little black imp,' cried Poll, 'that chuckles he-he-he?'

'That's the one,' muttered Charlee.

'What's his name, Charlee?' begged Poll. 'What's his name?'

She was sure the Curlew had brought her here for this. With the name on her tongue she could save the baby and Doll.

But Charlee did not answer. A mist was rising and blowing in off the sea, and when Poll looked at him it seemed also to rise in his eyes. After a long and anxious pause he shook his head.

'I've forgot,' he said. 'I did know. I've forgot.'

'Oh, it's too bad of you!' cried Poll in despair. 'Think, Charlee, think, think, think!'

Charlee stood like a stone, seeming to think, but the mist that dimmed the moonglade dimmed his wits.

'His name is lost in memory,' said Charlee.

'But you did know once,' urged Poll.

'Yes, I did know once.'

'And he does live in the Witching-Wood?'

'He's the black power of the Witching-Wood,' said Charlee.

Poll clenched her fists. 'Then I'm going to the Witching-Wood to find him.'

'You'd best give the go-by to the Witching-Wood,' muttered Charlee.

'That's what you always say,' said Poll, 'but this time I'm going.'

'There's ugly things come out of it,' said Charlee. 'Look you here.'

He went to his shack and kicked the rickety door ajar. On the inner side flapped a queer limp hide, as black as tar. Charlee fetched it off its nail and held it up between his two forefingers and thumbs, spreading its shape on the air.

'What is it?' asked Poll.

'One that was after my puffins a month gone by,' said Charlee. 'I felled it before it could hurt them, and dried its skin in the sun.'

'What for?'

'For something or other, how do I know?'

Poll looked at it closer and gave a little shudder. 'It looks just like the one that was after my Silver Curlew, and *did* hurt her.'

Charlee let the skin drop at his feet, saying, 'It's things like that you'll meet in the Witching-Wood. And if they catch sight of you I'm sorry for you.'

'I don't care,' said Poll, 'I'm going. I've got to find out that little black imp's name. I've *got* to, Charlee. If I don't, he'll have my sister and her baby for ever. See? I'm going,' she repeated, with a little tremble in her voice.

'Then I'll go too,' said Charlee, 'and heaven help us both.'

CHAPTER XV

In the Mist

ALL this time the Silver Curlew had been dipping about the shore as though she and they were strangers; but now she came fluttering towards them, and when her bright eye spied the crumpled black skin lying on the shingle she did a queer thing. With an air of disdain she picked it up in her beak, flew into the air, dangled it over Poll's head, and let it fall over her shoulders.

Poll shook it off with a little shudder. 'Ugh!' she said. 'What did you want to do that for?'

The Curlew merely returned to her dipping among the pools. But Charlee's eye grew suddenly as bright as the bird's, and he nodded to himself, muttering, 'Yes, I see. Yes, I see.'

'What do you see, Charlee?' asked Poll.

'I see the Curlew's reason.'

'I can't,' said Poll. 'I can't see anything very much. It's growing mistier and mistier.'

And so it was; a soft white mist was blowing in off the sea. It muffled the moonlight, and made Poll feel she must talk in a whisper.

'Come you here,' said Charlee. 'Come close.'

She came and stood beside him, and he talked in a hushed voice.

'Now listen, Pollee, and be a good little girl for once.'

'If you mean I'm not to go to the Witching-Wood ——' began Poll.

'I don't,' said Charlee. 'If you must, you must. I don't like it a bit, but if you're clever maybe you'll come to no harm. Slip off your frock.'

'What for?' asked Poll.

'Do as you're told,' said Charlee.

Poll pulled her cotton frock over her head and stood there in her vest. She felt the wisps of mist curling round her legs and arms, and shivered a little. She pretended to herself that she shivered because of the mysterious chilly feeling of the mist on her bare flesh, but it was due to something more mysterious still. The mist seemed to swallow up the world she knew,

and leave her standing on the shores of another life.

'Sit you down,' whispered Charlee.

Poll sat down on a boulder and Charlee knelt in front of her. He undid her sandals, drew her bare feet out straight, and then began to work the black animal skin up her legs. Poll made a face as he worked.

'Ugly,' muttered Charlee, 'yes I know, but it's little girls take harm in the Witching-Wood, not ugly things like this. You're just the size too, that's a bit of luck. That imp of mischief gathers queer things about him to amuse him and obey him and tickle his conceitedness. And so you'll go to find him like one of his own.'

'I won't obey him! I won't amuse him!' hissed Poll. 'I won't tickle his conceitedness.'

'Then you won't learn his name maybe,' said Charlee, wrinkling the skin up her body and along her arms.

'I see,' murmured Poll. 'Yes, *I* see now.' She thought of the baby, and let Charlee do what he would. She felt fierce and determined against the imp who wanted her baby. But suddenly she seemed to hear him chuckling again inside the bale of flax, and her fierceness dwindled in her, and she said in a small voice, 'Charlee.'

'Um?'

'Did you say—you did say, didn't you?'

'Say what?'

'You'd come too.'

'I'll come,' said Charlee. 'I'll lead you to the thick of the Witching-Wood, and I'll stay near. But that imp of darkness knows me, and if he catches sight of me nor you nor I will be worth the snuff of a candle. He knows me of old, and he knows I've killed his creatures. Stand you up.'

Poll stood. She was clothed in the black skin from head to foot. She felt ill at ease squeezed inside it, and when she moved her movements were no longer those of a limber little girl. They were awkward and ungainly. Charlee looked her slowly up and down.

'May do. May do,' he said.

Very carefully he drew the snouty black head over her hair.

'Charlee, Charlee! I can't see.'

'You'll soon find the eyeholes.'

'Charlee, Charlee! I can't breathe.'

'You'll come to it in a minute.'

'Charlee, Charlee! I'm lost,' cried poor Poll.

'Come you after me, come,' said Charlee Loon.

The mists were now so thick that sea and moon were invisible, and the Silver Curlew seemed drowned in rolling smoke. Poll could only see Charlee's shape dimly in front of her, and as it moved away fear gripped the little girl's heart.

'Charlee, don't go, don't go.'

'This way,' whispered Charlee.

'Don't go so fast.'

'Come you here,' his voice floated back to her through the mist.

She made her stiff black legs move after him, fearful of losing him. Sometimes she could not see him any more, and then she whispered, 'Char—lee! O—O! Chaar—lee!' as loud as she dared. And somewhere ahead of her the misty wind brought back his whisper, '*Polll—leee!*' and Poll followed it blindly. She was no longer treading on sand, but stumbling over twisted roots, through scratchy briars, and instead of the salty sea she smelled foul marsh-smells. She groped as best she could, and presently became too frightened to call to him, lest his name was heard by those who wished him ill. For now Poll knew she was in the Witching-Wood; she heard frogs croaking, and an adder hiss, and a harsh bird made a sound like a stick rattled

113

along a fence. The mist was thinner although the night was darker, and gradually Poll's eyes got used to the gloom, and she could even see a little where she was going. Charlee was now out of both sight and hearing. Only now and then came the faint pipe of his whistle, and she stumbled after it as best she could.

All of a sudden she was no longer alone in a strange world. There was a creaking of twigs, and through the undergrowth crept two little figures, not unlike her own. Before she knew what was happening they leapt upon her with shrill cries of triumph, and, each gripping one of her arms, they dragged her away.

CHAPTER XVI

The Witching-Wood

I N the heart of the Witching-Wood a crimson fire
glowed between two stout pine-trees, whose scaly
forms soared into the black night. From a chain
slung across them a huge black cauldron hung over
the red flames, which licked its sides as though they
longed to taste the steaming contents; but the smell
which rose with the steam would not have tempted
Abe and Sid and Dave and Hal Codling, accustomed
to smacking their lips over their mother's cookery.

The cook who stirred the big black pot was a woman with very different looks from that comfortable dame, and very different ideas about what was savoury for supper. She was lean and scraggy, with tangled grey tresses, and wispy hairs sprouting from her chin and cheeks and eyebrows. She was known as the Spider-Mother, and her name was Rackny. About her hopped and scrambled half a dozen of the Queer Things the Spindle-Imp liked to gather round him. Queer names they had too, such as Trimingham, Gimingham, Knapton and Trunch, and Northrepps and Southrepps; they slithered to and fro, or crouched and grubbed in the earth, bringing Rackny whatever they had found to go into the stew. The Spider-Mother's bony fingers clutched a long-handled iron spoon. Every now and then, after throwing something new into the pot, she stirred the mess vigorously, and dipped out a spoonful; and when she had tasted it she wagged her head with horrid satisfaction, and fell to stirring anew, singing meanwhile in a cracked and tuneless voice:

> *What have we got*
> *For the Master's pot*
> *When he calls for his bite and his booze?*
> *Serpents' eggs,*
> *And spiders' legs,*
> *And the dregs of the River Ouse.*
> *Ho! Ho!*
> *In they go!*
> *The best of savoury stews*
> *Is serpents' eggs,*

And spiders' legs,
And the muddy dregs
            of the Ouse!
Stir about, stir about,
Stir the black pot,
Boil till it bubbles
And serve it up hot.

'Bubble-ubble-ubble!' shrieked the Queer Things.

'Bubble-ubble-ubble!' snickered the fire.

'Bubble-ubble-ubble-ubble-ubble!' gurgled the pot.

The Queer Things capered with glee and rubbed their stomachs, and Rackny went on flinging in this and that. Presently she stopped as if petrified, and lifted one skinny finger to her ear.

'Hist! List! Whist!'

From somewhere far away came the sound of a tune on a whistle.

'Go see! go see!' hissed Rackny.

Trimingham and Gimingham instantly slithered away.

'Another pinch of henbane, Knapton,' said Rackny. 'More toadstools, Trunch, the rottener the better.'

They darted hither and thither, fetching what she required; and ever and anon she paused to cock her ear, and listen.

Before long Trimingham and Gimingham reappeared, dragging between them a little shape as peculiar as their own. Inside the hairy hide Poll's heart thumped so loud she thought they must hear it. It thumped still louder when she gazed on the eerie place

117

to which she had been brought. It seemed to be the chosen home of insects and nettles. Everything that could sting or prick was there. The two pine-trees looked like scaly alligators rearing up to devour her, the fire spat and spluttered as if determined to scorch her, and the smell from the black pot was so vile that Poll felt sure it was being brewed to poison her. Worse than these, were the two horrid little things that nipped her by the arms; and worst of all was the lanky-haired, skinny-fingered witch, who turned her sunken eyes on her and hissed,

'What's here? what's here? Speak, if you've got a tongue.'

Poll swallowed a lump in her throat and managed to answer, 'I've got a tongue—I think.'

'Never mind thinking,' croaked Rackny. 'Speak up!'

'But they're pinching me!' cried Poll in an angry voice. Trimingham and Gimingham were nipping her spitefully.

'Pinch 'em back, pinch 'em back,' chuckled Rackny.

'Oh, may I?' cried Poll. Never had an order pleased her more. Wrenching her arms away from her two tormentors, she pinched first one and then the other as hard as she could. They put their tails between their legs, ducked their heads, and ran away squealing, and Poll's heart began to revive a little. Things might be worse, if she were allowed to give as good as she got.

Rackny was nodding approval, and chuckling, 'I like your spirit, newcomer. You look like one of our sort.'

'That's what I want to be,' said Poll. 'I want to be one of you. Do you think he'll let me?'

'He? Who?' asked Rackny.

'*You* know—What's-his-name,' said Poll, hoping to trick Rackny into giving away the name of the Spindle-Imp.

But the old witch chuckled and croaked, 'Ha-ha, the master, "What's-his-name"! Well said, newcomer.'

'But I didn't say,' said Poll, concealing her disappointment.

'And you did well not to. We never say the Master's name. You'll do, you'll do, so you can pass the test.'

'What test?' asked Poll, trying not to sound as anxious as she felt.

'Sometimes it's one thing, sometimes it's another. All newcomers must pass a test before they're let in. Nobody serves the Master who fails to pass. But you're in luck, newcomer, you come at a good moment. It happens we're one short, and there's room for you.'

'How come you to be one short?' asked Poll.

'Through that nasty Loon on the sea-shore who caught our little Runton,' snarled Rackny. She rubbed her red-rimmed eyes with her skinny fingers, stared hard at Poll, and muttered, 'Now I come to look at you, you're very like our little Runton, newcomer.'

'He—he was a sort of cousin of mine,' stammered Poll, hoping this explanation would satisfy the witch.

It seemed to do so, for she waggled her head again. 'Same snout,' she said.

'It runs in the family,' said Poll.

'Well then,' said Rackny, 'Runton shall be *your* name.'

'What's yours?' asked Poll.

'Rackny,' said the Spider-Mother.

'Rackny!' Poll nudged her slyly. 'Don't you sometimes long to say the Master's name? Just for fun?'

'Long to or not, Runton, it wouldn't be fun.'

'Just once,' coaxed Poll. 'Come on!'

'What are you getting at?' said Rackny suspiciously. 'It's more than my old skin's worth. Or yours, young Runton.'

'Oh dear!' thought Poll. 'Perhaps I can *sneer* her into it.' In her most contemptuous voice she said aloud, 'You *are* a coward, aren't you!'

'I care for my skin,' said Rackny. 'Nobody says his name except himself.'

'Then he *does* say it sometimes?' said Poll eagerly.

'When he's extra pleased with himself,' nodded Rackny. 'He'll be extra pleased with himself tonight when he comes again, bringing a fair mistress with him. Ah! and who d'ye think?'

'How should I know?' scowled Poll, who knew only too well.

'No less than the Queen of Norfolk!' chuckled Rackny cracking her bony knuckles.

'Never!' said Poll, longing to wring the Spider-Mother's wrinkled neck.

'Ah. He's gone away to fetch her. He'll be in a merry mood when he comes again. You're in luck, little Runton, he'll not make the test too hard for you,

and when you're one of us there'll be such junketings!
Fetch pine-cones. Feed the fire.'

Poll darted here and there, her eyes burning, her
heart full of anger, gathering handfuls of dry cones
and spindly needles which she threw among the flames
under the pot. They crickled and crackled, the pot
boiled and bubbled, and the horrible odour of the
steam made Poll shudder, and Rackny smack her lips
with anticipation. She plunged her iron ladle into the
cauldron, dipped out a spoonful, and swallowed the
boiling mess with gurgles of ecstasy.

'Dee-licious!' pronounced the hag, wriggling with
pleasure. 'Want a taste?'

Before she could draw back, Poll found a spoonful
tipped into her mouth.

'Dee-licious!' she echoed, and turning her back on
Rackny managed to spit it out.

'More?' asked Rackny. ''Tisn't everybody I'd cos-
set, but I've taken a fancy to you.'

'One mustn't spoil a good treat,' said Poll, wiping
her mouth with a handful of grass. 'I'd rather wait
till supper-time. What is it?'

'Serpents' eggs,' mumbled Rackny, 'and spiders'
legs, and the dregs of the muddy Ouse. Feed the fire,
little Runton, feed the fire.' Suddenly she stretched
her lean neck, and the grey hairs on her chin bristled
with excitement. 'Hist! list! whist! the Master's
coming!'

A clatter of wheels became audible. Poll's heart
thumped so hard that she could scarcely breathe.

Bumping and swaying through the trees came a ramshackle chariot, made up of old bones and draped with spiderwebs that blew in tatters about the black shape of the Spindle-Imp perched on a pivot in the middle. The vehicle was drawn by a team of eight bats, and it was attended by a small host of Queer Things that flapped and capered around it. As it rolled, the pivot twirled, and the Imp whizzed round and round on his pointed seat, his red-hot eyes glowing in his coal-black face. In his hand he held, instead of a whip, a long writhing grass-snake, with which he lashed out at the Things on either side of the chariot.

'Dance! dance! dance!' he hissed. 'Dance, Trimingham! Dance, Gimingham! Dance, Knapton and

Trunch! Northrepps! Southrepps! Dance all of a bunch! Caper, come caper, come caper!'

With flappings and caperings, hissings and whizzings, rattlings and clatterings, slashings and lashings, the chariot at last fetched up by the fire and the pivot stopped twizzling.

'Broth, Spider-Mother, broth!' commanded the Imp.

Rackny snatched up an ancient tortoise's shell, filled it with stew, and brought it to her master. He flickered his tongue over it, and his eyes shot sparks of satisfaction.

'Tasty! tasty!' he said, pinching Rackny's ear as a sign of favour. Taking the shell in both hands, he tilted and lapped it clean.

'I brewed broth for two, Master,' said the hag, 'Where is the Mistress?'

'All in good time, Spider-Mother, yew shall see her all in good time, and her little baby tew. I've gi'en the Queen a second chance, becos of her pretty little baby. Tewmorrow she must guess my name in three, or I'll have the pair of 'em, he-he-he! More broth.'

Rackny waggled her bony finger at Poll, who could scarcely contain herself for fury, as the Imp boasted and chuckled; but she was obliged to come forward and take the empty shell from the hag's hands, and fill it again from the cauldron, while the Imp chuckled on,

'And she woon't guess my name, she woon't, she woon't, she woon't!'

This was too much for Poll. 'Oh no, of course not!' she burst out angrily. 'You're so clever, aren't you?'

'I am, I am,' agreed the Imp. He fixed his glowing eyes on her for a terrible minute, during which Poll feared they would burn through her disguise. Then, turning to Rackny, he demanded, 'What's that there?'

''Tis the cousin of our poor little Runton,' said the Spider-Mother. 'It wants to be one of us.'

The Imp puffed up his chest like a pouter-pigeon. 'That thinks I'm clever, hey? And that'd like to serve me?'

'I'd jolly well like to serve you right!' cried Poll, exasperated by the horrid thing's conceit.

'Yew'll be jolly well sorry if yew serve me wrong,' snarled the Imp. 'What's yar name?'

'Runton,' said Poll. 'What's yours?'

'He, he, he! yew're clever tew, hain't ye?' chortled the Imp. He tweaked her ear as he had tweaked Rackny's and went on, 'But yew hain't so clever as me. Nobody under the moon's so clever as me.' He jumped down from his pivot and began to strut up and down in front of her, twirling his tail madly. 'What d'yew think of me, hey?'

'There's no words in the dictionary,' said Poll, 'to tell you what I think of you.'

This made the Imp strut more than ever; he swelled so that his skin became as tight as a drum. 'No words in the dictionary, he, he, he!' he chortled. Then suddenly he let down his chest a little, and eyed Poll suspiciously. '*What* dictionary?' he asked. 'Dew yew mean a *little* dictionary, dew yew?'

'I mean a *big* dictionary,' said Poll.

'*How* big?'

'The biggest you ever saw.'

'In one volume?' asked the Imp craftily.

'In twenty volumes!' cried Poll.

This seemed to satisfy him, and he began once more to strut and swell and twirl his tail. 'D'yew hear that, Spider-Mother? There hain't words in twenty volumes to describe what Runton thinks of me. Good, Runton! so far good. But now,' said he, resuming his seat on the pivot, 'now I must set yew the test.'

'What sort of test?' asked Poll, trying to put a bold face on it. But to tell the truth, she dreaded what was coming.

'That's a riddle test, to test the powers of yar wits,' said the Imp. 'If yar's witty, yew'll become one of us. If yar hain't, into the pot yew goo!'

'*Into—the—pot?*' quavered Poll.

'If yew doon't guess my riddle,' said the Imp, rubbing his hands.

'But nobody,' objected Poll, 'nobody *ever* guesses riddles. It's not fair.'

This brought the Imp down from his perch in a flaming temper. He advanced on Poll, twirling his tail in her face, and screaming, 'Not fair? Not fair? Dew yew dare tew say I'm not fair?'

Poll retreated before him; she was very frightened, but was even angrier, and she managed to spit back, 'Fair? You? Oh yes, you're as fair as—as snow in a coal-mine, and—and salt in a black pudding.'

'D'yew hear that, Spider-Mother?' crowed the Imp.

125

'Snow and salt, that's how fair I be.' And he twirled in glee of what he took for a compliment.

'But just the same,' persisted Poll, 'people *always* give riddles up.'

'Yew give up my riddle,' said the Imp, 'and into the pot yew goo, as sure as my name is——'

'What?' asked Poll quickly. 'As sure as your name is *what*?'

Was she going to catch him? She held her breath. But——

'That'd be telling,' sniggered the Imp. 'Noo then, are yew ready?'

'Yes,' said poor Poll faintly, 'I'm ready.'

'Then here's my riddle,' said the Imp. But before he spoke it, he twirled like a teetotum, till Poll's eyes grew dizzy, and her thoughts even dizzier; and if ever she had a chance of thinking clearly, it was completely lost as the Imp stopped sharply, and pointing a black finger at her pronounced:

> *Hannibal Jones was fond of eggs,*
> *His breakfast every day was eggs,*
> *He kept no chickens who laid his eggs,*
> *He bought no eggs, he borrowed no eggs,*
> *He stole no eggs and was given no eggs.*
> *How did Hannibal Jones get eggs?*

To make things worse, as soon as the Imp finished, Trimingham, Gimingham, Knapton, Trunch, Northrepps, and Southrepps and all the tribe of Queer Things starting whirling round and round, squeaking and grunting, according to their kind:

Poll drew a deep breath to steady herself, and hoping to gain time repeated slowly, 'How—did—Hannibal—Jones—get—eggs?'

'He, he, he!' chuckled the Imp; and 'He, he, he!' echoed the Queer Things, encircling her and pointing malicious fingers, once more demanding at the tops and the bottoms of their voices:

'How did Hannibal Jones get eggs?'

'Give us a minute,' said poor bewildered Poll. 'Can I recap?'

'Goo ahead,' sneered the Imp.

'Nobody gave Hannibal Jones eggs?' asked Poll.

'Nobody,' said the Imp.

'And he didn't steal them?' asked Poll.

'Never,' said the Imp.

'Or borrow them?' asked Poll.

'Not he,' said the Imp.

'Or buy them?' asked Poll.

'Ne'er a one,' said the Imp.

'And you're quite sure,' asked Poll, 'he didn't keep chickens?'

'Noo!' said the Imp. 'He didn't keep chickens, he, he, he! Hannibal Jones kept no chickens at all.'

'But he *did* have eggs for breakfast, *every day*?' persisted Poll.

'Ivery day of his life,' agreed the Imp. 'And for tea tew.'

Poll put her hands to her head. She tried not to let

them see that she was reduced to desperation. The Imp twirled his tail, and asked, in a tone of satisfaction,

'Dew yew give it up?'

'Give it up? Give it up?' squealed and growled the Queer Things.

Poll faltered, 'I—— I——' And nothing more would come.

'Runton's going to give it up,' sniggered Rackny.

Up went the yell: 'Into the pot with Runton!'

Poll retreated terrified before the rush they made at her, retreated till she could retreat no more, because one of the tall pine-trees stopped the way. When she felt its hard rough trunk like an iron bar against her back, and heard the crackling of the fire that burned beside it, and smelt the steam of the pot into which she was to be cast, she closed her eyes and gave herself up for lost. And just at that minute, from behind the tree, she heard a tiny sound, the sound of Charlee's pipe, so soft that it was no more than the merest whisper. But beyond all doubt it was the pipe of her friend, and she knew that he was near, as he had promised to be.

'Save me!' she murmured under her breath. 'Save me, Charlee!'

The pipe stopped playing, and she listened with all her might, through the racket made by the gleeful horrid Things pressing upon her. What she heard was simply:

Quack-quack! Quack-quack!

It was enough! The sound was lost among the harsh shrill noises made by the Queer Things, if they heard it at all they would only have taken it for one of their own croakings; but for Poll, it was enough to tell her the answer to the riddle.

As the Queer Things, yelling again, 'Into the pot with Runton!' made a rush at her, she dodged them, broke through their clutching hands, and faced the Imp defiantly.

'Touch me if you dare!' cried Poll. 'Your riddle's as easy as pie! Quack-quack! HANNIBAL JONES KEPT DUCKS. Quack-quack! He didn't have to keep chickens, he had ducks-eggs for breakfast and tea, quack-quack, quack-quack!'

'*Qua-qua-qua!*' shrieked the Queer Things.

'*Quee-quee-quee!*' screamed Rackny.

'Well done, little Runton!' chuckled the Imp.

Then all the company broke into a raucous song.

> *Qua-qua-qua!*
> *Quee-quee-quee!*
> *Hannibal Jones wants eggs for tea.*
> *Qua-qua-qua!*
> *Quee-quee-quee!*
> *For breakfast and supper and dinner and tea.*
> *He likes them hard, he likes them soft,*
> *He likes them poached and he likes them oft!*
> *He likes them in omelettes,*
> *He likes them in custard,*
> *As white as salt*
> *And as yellow as mustard,*
> *He likes them coddled and scrambled and fried,*
> *And best of all he likes them inside!*

QUA! QUA!

Quee-quee-quee!
Hannibal Jones wants eggs for tea.
Down, ducks, on your waddling legs,
And lay your eggs, and lay your eggs!
Downy ducks, duck down on your bones,
You can't lay too many for Hannibal Jones!

As they finished the song, all the Queer Things squatted down on their haunches, and when they rose up again, there in each place lay a large creamy egg. Fearing lest she should be expected to do the same, Poll hastily gathered them all up and presented them to the Imp, who cracked them, one after the other, and tossed the contents down his throat. Then, much to her disgust, he patted Poll on the head and announced,

'Runton is one of us! Runton's a witty one, Runton is, as sure as my name is——'

'What? As sure as your name is *what*?' asked Poll again. Next moment she could have bitten her tongue out, for the Imp pulled himself up, wagged his finger at her, and chuckled,

'He, he, he! That'd be telling, that would. Yew don't catch *me*, little Runton! Up with yew, Runton, and show me how yew can dance!'

So saying he twirled himself off his perch and leapt into their midst, and they all broke into a wild capering dance, while Rackny beat time with her iron spoon on the pot. The Imp had Poll fast by the hand, and as he leapt and sank, twisted round and round, and wove his way in and out of the throng, she had to leap and sink, twist and weave after him, till her heart thumped against her ribs, and she staggered for want of breath.

'Dance, Runton, dance!' screamed the Imp, and taking her by the shoulders he shook her backwards and forwards with all his might. The violence of his movements jerked the disguise that covered her head, and to her horror the animal snout dropped back, and Poll was left panting on the ground, with her hair falling over her shoulders.

The dancing forms about her stopped as still as if they had been frozen.

'That's a child!' snarled the Imp.

'That's a child!' echoed the Queer Things.

'That isn't Runton at all,' hissed Rackny, 'that's a horrid—little—girl!'

The Queer Things set up their howl: 'To the pot! To the pot!' and Poll gave herself up for lost.

But Rackny held up a finger. 'Hist! list! whist!'— and a clear little piping tune, a silver rain of notes, began to trickle through the ugly croakings that had filled Poll's heart with terror. In the silence that fell as the last few notes trembled away like scattering dew from a flower, Polly, unable to stop herself, sang out: 'Char—lee! Chaar—leeee!' and her heart leapt for joy to hear him sing back his long-drawn-out: 'Poll—ee! Poll—leee!'

The Queer Things were crouched as still as cats before they pounce.

'Come quick, come quick!' she cried faintly; then,

realizing the terrible fate in store for her friend as well as for herself, she called again with all her strength: 'No, no, don't come, don't come!'

'I've come,' said Charlee, stepping through the trees to her side.

Poll did not know if she was glad or sorry. She heard the Imp snarl, 'It's the Loon!' She saw the Queer Things creeping closer and closer in the red firelight, echoing in a mutter, 'The Loon! We've got the Loon!'

Then they pounced.

Poll shut her eyes very tight, prepared for the worst. Oh, why had she called for help? Why had she let Charlee risk his life with hers? And why—— Why didn't she feel the crooked fingers of the Queer Things clutching at her?

Mysterious music was weaving through her ears. She opened her eyes a little, and saw that the music came from Charlee's pipe, music such as she had never heard him play before, music so still that it seemed hardly to move, so cold that it felt like frost upon the air, so dreamy that you could not believe you were awake. It was like no music ever heard on earth. 'The moon,' thought Poll, 'it must be the sort of music they play in the moon.' Each note created a shimmering veil of mist that hung between Poll and Charlee and the dark wood; and in the darkness beyond the light she could see the Queer Things crouched as if petrified in the uncouth positions in which they had gathered themselves to spring.

And now strange words seemed to swim through the pipe with the tune, but whether Charlee was breathing them as he blew, or whether the moon-misty notes had a tongue of their own, Poll could not have said.

'*Malchus* . . .' breathed the pipe. '*Martinian* . . . *Serapion* . . .'.

The Queer Things swayed like shadows, and Rackny yawned.

> *The Spell of the Seven Sleepers* (breathed the pipe)
> *I put upon your peepers,*
> *The sevenfold spell of the Sleepers*
> *In Ephesus long gone.*
> *Malchus . . . Maximinian . . .*
> *Dionysius . . . John . . .*
> *Constantine . . . Martinian . . .*
> *And Serapion. . . .*

What did the strange spell mean? But what did it matter? The Queer Things were nodding now, their misshapen heads flopping from side to side, their heavy eyelids lolling up and down. Rackny's skinny arms stretched till they seemed twice their length, like a spider uncurling its legs.

'*Maximinnnian* . . .' breathed the pipe. '*Dionysssiusss* . . . *Connnstantine* . . .'.

One by one the Queer Things sank to the ground beneath the spell of the pipe.

Only the Spindle-Imp remained immune. The spell had no power over him, and he twirled with fury as he saw his creatures going down softly among the pine-needles, his eyes shot sparks like red-hot cinders from a sputtering coal, and waving his malevolent black arms he began to set his spell against the Loon's.

The spell of the Spider-Spinners
Weaving from their inners,
The spidery spell of the spinners
About your limbs I bind!
Securely shall they bind you
Against the piney rind,
Where nobody shall find you
Except the wailing wind.

Two huge spiders dropped out of the pine-branches in mid-air, and while the Spindle-Imp chanted they swiftly span their silk about Poll and Charlee Loon. Before they could resist, each was drawn close against one of the pine-tree trunks, and their limbs were bound round and round with the spider-silk, finer than hair and stronger than steel. But until his arms were bound, Charlee continued to breathe his spell.

'*Malchus . . . Maximinian . . .*'.

'Bind 'em! bind 'em! wind 'em!' snarled the Imp.

'*Dionysius . . . John . . .*' whistled the Loon.

'Wind 'em! wind 'em! bind 'em!' snarled the Imp.

'*Constantine . . .*' sang the pipe. '*Martinian . . .*'.

'None shall hear or find 'em!' sneered the Imp.

'*Serapion . . .*' sang the pipe. '*Serapion . . .*'.

And at each strange name a Queer Thing fell asleep. Last of all fell Rackny.

'Two hundred nine-and-twenty years shall you lie there,' murmured Charlee to the sleepers.

134

'Just so long shall yew and she stand there, Loon!'
snarled the Imp. 'In time unborn all these shall come
agen, when yew two shall be bones, bones, bones!'

A little streak of light began to glow beyond the
trees. The long strange night was coming to an end.

'Sun-up!' cried the Imp, twirling with triumph.
'The day of the Christening. Tom Tit Tot 'll be there,
Tom Tit Tot 'll be there!'

'Tom Tit Tot!' gasped Poll.

At last, at last he had given himself away! At last he
had spoken his name! But much he cared! Crouching

beside her, as she struggled vainly in her bonds, the Imp jeered in her ear:

'Nimmy-nimmy-not, my name is Tom Tit Tot! Much good may it dew yew, my little dear.'

With that he swung his tail over his arm, and capered round her croaking:

> *Tom Tit Tot!*
> *Tom Tit Tot!*
> *Nimmy-nimmy-not*
> *My name is TOM TIT TOT!*

He twirled himself out of sight through the trees.

CHAPTER XVII

The Curlew Flies

So now Poll knew his name! She knew the name she had promised Doll to discover, the name that would save both Doll and her baby, if only—*if only* she could get to the palace before the guessing began.

She tried in vain to wriggle out of her bonds. Couldn't Charlee help? But when she looked across at his tree the magic seemed to have gone out of him; he stood as still as a stone in his bonds while Poll writhed and twisted in hers. Oh, who could have dreamed that spider-thread was so strong, however many strands of it there were?

'Charlee, Charlee!' she cried. 'His name is Tom Tit Tot! Oh Charlee! his name is Tom Tit Tot!'

'Much good may it do us,' said Charlee.

But if Poll called it very very loud, couldn't she make her sister hear it somehow?

'Doll! Doll! Doll! His name is Tom Tit Tot! *Tom—Tit—Tot!* Can you hear me, Doll? His name is Tom—Tit—Tot!'

No, Doll, miles and miles away, would never hear her, she would never know. Doll would not hear, even if Poll's voice were not strangled with her tears. She broke down and sobbed, continuing to whisper, 'His name is Tom Tit Tot.'

In the east the streak of morning grew a little brighter. Soon the christening bells would start chiming all over Norfolk, and in Norwich Cathedral the Bishop would be putting on his mitre to give the baby the name Doll had chosen for it. But the baby would never get its name now, because of the name Doll would never be able to guess.

> *Nimmy-nimmy-not*
> *My name is Tom Tit Tot.*

Exhausted with crying, Poll's hoarse little voice could scarcely whisper it now. The sun was rising, and hope had gone out of the world. But surely, surely hope should rise with the sun?

Something was happening. What? Poll lifted her wet face, and through a blur of tears she saw bright wings come sailing down the day.

'Curlew!' she whispered. 'Curlew—Silver Curlew!'

The Curlew alighted at a little distance. As usual she seemed not to notice anything much. Picking her dainty disdainful way among the sleeping Things, she danced for her own pleasure in the sun. Never, never had she looked so lovely. Her long curved beak was like an arc of light, her silver plumage was ruffled with pale gold, she stepped delicately among the pine-needles, spread and shut her gleaming wings, rose a little, flew a little, came down to earth, and stood preening her feathers. Poll watched each movement eagerly. She couldn't have come for nothing, she couldn't *not* know Charlee and Poll were there: Charlee who had mended her broken wing, Poll who had nursed her tenderly for a year. But what does a bird know? What does a bird feel? What matters to a bird but its own purpose?

'Curlew, my Curlew,' pleaded little Poll.

Surely the Curlew heard and understood! She stepped to the pine, and with her slender beak pecked negligently for a moment at Poll's bonds. She soon gave it up, and skirting the dying fire stood before Charlee's tree with her head on one side.

'Peck away,' said Charlee, 'peck away.'

But after a peck or so the Curlew went away again to preen herself.

'Too much for her, I reckon,' muttered the Loon.

'Must we stand here till we're bones?' said Poll. 'Must Tom Tit Tot get our baby?'

The Curlew spread her wings to fly away.

139

'She's going, she's going!' cried Poll in desperation. 'Oh Curlew, please don't go!'

It seemed to her that the last ray of hope would vanish with the bird. She was already poised upon the air.

Suddenly Charlee Loon launched out with his foot. At the edge of the fire by his tree glowed a half-burnt twig. With an effort he managed to kick it clear of the ashes. The wind of the movement fanned it into a flame; it lay flickering on the ground like a little goldfish.

The Curlew saw it, and hovered in her flight. Then, as though she were dipping for her breakfast in the sea, she darted down and caught the dead end of the twig in her beak. Almost before they realized her purpose, she had flown behind the pine-trees and applied the flame first to Poll's and then to Charlee's bonds. The fire did what she had lacked the strength to do; it burned through the knots her beak could not untie, and the Loon and the little girl stood free in the Witching-Wood.

For one moment Poll stood dazed, rubbing her wrists. Then—'Run, Charlee, run, Charlee, run!'

She ran and ran and ran to get out of the wood. She had only one thought, to reach the palace in time. So she did not see the Loon run the other way, or the Silver Curlew disappear in the dawn.

CHAPTER XVIII

'*We'll never be Ready in Time!*'

Yes, the bells were beginning to chime now for the Christening. All over Norfolk they rang from every steeple, and in every home people scrambled out of bed to make themselves ready for the road to Norwich. Well, not quite everybody; but those who were not within walking or riding distance of the Cathedral were preparing their own jollifications in honour of the royal baby. Flags flew over town halls and village schools; churches were filled with flowers, innkeepers stood treat to all comers, squires gave golden pennies to their tenants' children, carthorses wore rosettes as if they were Prize Turkeys, parlours were decorated as if Christmas had come again, cakes and pies were baking in every oven, and every girl in Norfolk was wearing something new: a new hat, a new dress, a new apron, a new pair of slippers. Those who were too poor to buy even a new hair-ribbon ran out to the fields and picked a bunch of moon-daisies to tuck in their bodices.

But the hustle and bustle throughout the County was as nothing compared with the hustle and bustle in the Palace itself. Everybody was doing something to something that somebody had done the day before; and whatever they were doing seemed as if it would never get done. They rushed hither and thither

141

exclaiming, 'Hurry, hurry, hurry! We shall never be ready in time!'

Mother Codling was re-ironing the muslin Christening-robe that was already as crisp as a spring lettuce.

Megs was rearranging all the flowers in all the vases that already looked as pretty as pictures.

Jen was repolishing the fire-irons that were already as bright as new pins.

Cookie was baking an extra batch of gingerbread boys with currant eyes, as if seven-thousand-seven-hundred-and-seventy-seven weren't already more than enough.

Abe and Sid and Dave and Hal had rushed to the linen-draper's to buy yellow ties with blue horseshoes on them in place of the red ties with green stirrups which Mother Codling had bought them only yesterday, and were tying them round each other's collars and changing their minds about them every other minute.

'We'll never be Ready in Time!'

The Gardener had suddenly decided to weed the onion-bed, because he couldn't think of anything else to do, and had got his nails full of dirt, and was trying to trim them with the garden-shears after trying to clean them with the dibble.

The Butler had gone down to the cellar to fetch up another dozen dozen of sparkling cider, and had got cobwebs in his hair, and couldn't find his brush and comb.

Nollekens was bursting into the Nursery every other minute, to complain of something or other and burst out again.

And Doll? What was Doll doing? She was kneeling at the window with her chin in her hands, gazing into the distance, and whispering under her breath, 'Oh Poll, Poll, Poll! come quick!'

'Owch!' shrieked Mother Codling. She had been holding the flat-iron to her cheek to see if it was too hot for the baby-muslin, and it was. So she dropped it on the carpet where it made a round hole and a scorchy smell. 'Flour!' cried Mother Codling, clapping her hand to her cheek.

'Here you are!' cried Megs, snatching a handful of roses from a vase on the mantelpiece, which fell down and was smashed to bits among Jen's fire-irons. Jen dropped her polishing-rag, Megs clapped the roses to Mother Codling's hand, and Mother Codling's hand boxed Meg's ear.

'Not *Flower*, stoopid, FLOUR!' bawled Mother Codling.

'Why can't you say what you mean?' asked Megs. 'Look at all the mess you've made me make.'

'Look at all these thorn-pricks on my arm,' retorted Mother Codling. 'If you had to plaster me all over with flowers, why not petunias?'

'Because there aren't any,' said Megs. 'Get some petunias,' she told the Gardener, coming in with his shears.

'What for?' he asked. 'Can you lend me some fingernail-scissors?'

'No I can't, and Mother Codling wants to put some petunias on her face, but for goodness sake don't ask me why.'

'It's a curious thing,' said the Gardener, 'that shears is good for trimming hedges, but no manner of good for fingernails. There ain't no petunias in the greenhouse.'

'I wouldn't want petunias if there were,' snapped Mother Codling. 'I never did want petunias. I only said why not?'

'Why not indeed,' agreed the Gardener. 'And also why?'

'Never you mind,' said Mother Codling. 'All I ask is a handful of flour, and not self-raising neither.'

'I'll get some un-self-raising flour from Cookie,' said Jen; she had been trying to wipe up the broken vase with her rag, but now she dropped it again and rushed down to the kitchen.

'Who's got a clothes-brush?' asked the Butler, coming in with his arms full of bottles and his hair full of cobwebs.

'Can you lend me some fingernail-scissors?' asked the Gardener. 'What might you want a clothes-brush for?'

'To brush my hair with,' said the Butler. 'I don't use scissors, I use a file.'

'I can't see no clothes in your hair,' said the Gardener, looking.

'Well, there aren't any,' said the Butler.

'Then what do you want a clothes-brush for?' asked the Gardener again.

'I've rather forgotten,' said the Butler. 'What might you want with scissors?'

'I don't quite remember,' said the Gardener.

Jen came running back with a handful of ground ginger. 'Cookie says she's used up all the flour, and has anyone seen her duffle cloak, and will this do instead?'

'I don't see how ground ginger will do instead of a duffle cloak in any circumstances whatsoever,' said Mother Codling. 'So I shall go and put on my Sunday toque, or we'll never be ready in time.'

'If we comes in late,' said Abe, 'the people'll stare.'

'And the bellringers glare!' said Sid.

'The verger will tear the remains of his hair,' said Dave.

'And the lady in flat-footed shoes will despair,' said Hal.

'What lady in flat-footed shoes?' asked the Gardener.

'The one who opens the pews,' said Hal.

'I suppose she could wear high heels if she wanted

to,' said the Gardener. 'What's *she* got to despair about, I'd like to know?'

'She's got bunions,' said Hal.

'Some people are never satisfied,' said the Gardener.

'Oh, do stop argufying,' cried Mother Codling. 'Where *have* I been and gone and put my Sunday toque? We shall *never* be ready in time.'

'Has anyone seen my bag?' asked old Nan, waddling in.

'There, Nanny's lost her bag now,' groaned Megs.

'This,' said the Butler, 'is the camel's back. Where did you have it last, Nanny?'

'Down in the basement, and it isn't there now. No! don't all start rushing down as if I didn't know what I'm talking about—I tell you it's somewhere else.'

'We all know what bags are,' said the Butler, wiping the cobwebs out of his hair with Jen's rag. 'You leave 'em down in the basement and find 'em in the attic. Peripatetic, that's bags.'

'Mine is mock Morocco,' said old Nan, 'so now you know what to look for.'

'There isn't *time*,' objected Mother Codling.

'There's *got* to be time,' said old Nan. 'I can't possibly go to Church without my bag.'

'Why not?'

'It's got all my Things in it. Look for it, everybody.'

Everybody rushed here and there, looking. The Butler looked up the chimney, the Gardener looked

in the coal-scuttle, Abe bumped into Sid, Sid bumped
into Dave, Dave bumped into Hal, and Hal bumped
into Nollekens, who came into the room shouting,

'Who has taken my sealing-wax?'

'What's the matter with *you*?' asked Nanny sharply.

'Somebody's taken my sealing-wax. It *was* there
and now it *isn't*. It was *red* sealing-wax, and somebody's taken it. It was all blobby and glisteny. I
bought it yesterday for tuppence, and I've only used
it *once*. My beautiful sealing-wax!' Nollekens stamped
his foot. 'Isn't anybody *listening*?'

Cookie came in, dusting flour and ginger off her
stout arms.

'Where's my sealing-wax?' demanded Nollekens.

'Don't ask *me*. I'm looking for my duffle cloak.'

Nollekens made a rush at the Butler, who was
picking bits of broken vase out of his hair. *'Where—
is—my—*SEALING-WAX?'

The Butler said coldly, 'I'm not in the habit of
stealing wax what doesn't belong to me.'

'What do you want with sealing-wax at a Christening
anyhow?' asked Cookie.

'Well,' said Nollekens sulkily, 'you might want to
seal *some*thing. You never know.'

'True,' said Abe. 'You never know.'

'Yes, you never do, do you?' said Sid.

'No,' said Dave, 'you never don't.'

'What don't you never?' asked Hal.

But by this time they had forgotten, and Nollekens
had rushed away and come back waving a blue sock

with white dots in one hand and a red sock with white stripes in the other.

'Just *look* what the laundry has been and sent home!' he shouted. 'Look Nanny! I *can't* go to the Christening in an odd pair of socks.'

'I *shan't* go without my duffle cloak!' cried Cookie.

'I *don't* go without my Sunday toque!' vowed Mother Codling.

'I *won't*, I positively will NOT go without my bag!' said old Nan firmly.

And with one voice they all cried together:

'We'll *never* be ready in time.'

In and out and round about they scurried, trying to find their lost things, to tidy up the messes, to tidy up themselves, to recover their breath, and their wits, and their tempers.

Only Doll, who had taken no part in the fluster, and seemed scarcely to have noticed it, was left alone at the window, whispering again and again:

'Poll, Poll, Poll! come quick!'

CHAPTER XIX

The Worst Spinster in Norfolk

COMING back into the Nursery to finish cleaning up the hearth, Jen saw two tears rolling down Doll's cheeks. How strange, thought Jen, that someone with a King for a husband and a Princess for a baby, should ever cry.

'What is it, Queen Doll?' she asked.

'Jen, Jen! where's my little sister?'

'Gone down to the beach, most like,' said Jen, 'to get trash for her curlew.'

'Her curlew's flown,' said Doll, 'and my sister's gone, and I must face the day alone.'

'A happy day, Queen Doll,' said Jen, 'it's a *happy* day for every soul in Norfolk.'

'Except for me,' sighed Doll, 'except for me.'

'What is it, Queen Doll, oh what *is* it?' asked Jen again.

'I want my little sister,' whispered Doll.

This seemed to bring their talk round to where it began, and before Jen could think of what to say next, Nollekens strutted in in a splendid cloak of red velvet embroidered with gold cricket-bats.

'Are you ready, Dollikins?' he asked. '*I'm* ready.' He twirled himself about, making the mantle fly out on all sides. 'Do you like my new cloak?'

'It's very fine,' said Doll, gazing out of the window.

'And my shoe-buckles, do you like my shoe-buckles?' Nollekens stuck up first one foot then the other, so that the buckles caught the glitter from the sun.

'Magnificent,' said Doll, still gazing out of the window.

'But are they *bright* enough, do you think?' asked Nollekens. 'Give them a rub-up, Jen.' He put his foot on the fender, and Jen gave the buckles a polish with her rag. Nollekens's temper had quite passed off, and he was now feeling as pleased as Punch with himself and all the world. 'Would you like to see what I'm giving our infant for a Christening-present, Doll? I've spent ever such a lot of thought on it. Shall I show it to you?'

'If you please.' Doll came away from the window and stood beside him.

'Here it is then.' He tugged a handsome leather case out of his pocket.

'That'll be a pearl necklace,' said Jen admiringly.

Doll opened the case and looked inside. 'It's a set of razor-blades!'

'Seven!' said Nollekens proudly. 'One for each day of the week. Aren't they splendid!'

'Razors are of no use to our child,' said Doll.

'Not *yet* perhaps,' said Nollekens petulantly, 'but they will be one day. He can lend them to me till he's ready.'

'Our child is a girl,' said Doll.

'*Is* he?' said Nollekens. 'Why didn't somebody tell

me? Well then, I'll have to keep the razors myself. Isn't that lucky?' He stuffed the case back lovingly into his pocket. 'What are *you* giving him, Doll?'

'Nothing,' she said.

'How funny of you,' said Nollekens. 'But p'raps he won't notice. It's time we were off. Pop on your bonnet, Dollikins, and come to church.'

'I'm not coming,' said Doll.

Nollekens stared at her with his mouth open. '*You're—not—coming?*'

'I'm not coming to church till Poll gets home.'

'But that's nonsense, you know.'

'It isn't, it's sense.'

'Why?'

'She's gone to find out,' said Doll.

'What?' asked Noll.

'I don't know,' said Doll.

'Where?' asked Noll.

'I don't know,' said Doll.

'When will she be back?' asked Noll.

'I don't know,' said Doll.

'You don't seem to know anything,' said Nollekens.

Doll only said, 'I know I must wait for Poll.'

'Well, *I* shan't,' said Nollekens. 'It's not *her* Christening. Where *is* everybody?'

He snatched a big muffin-bell off the table, where he always kept it handy in case he wanted muffins. Instantly the Nursery was full of bustling people again, for it was understood that whenever Nollekens rang that bell he mustn't be kept waiting. Mother Codling came in tying the ribbons of her Sunday toque, which had been found perched on the breast of a plump capon under a dish-cover in the boxroom; and she was explaining to everybody how she had just remembered putting the bonnet on the capon to keep out the flies, and putting the dish-cover on the bonnet to keep out the dust, and shutting them up in the boxroom to keep out the boys. Abe and Sid and Dave and Hal were making bow-knots of their ties, and were wearing two ties apiece, because they couldn't make up their minds between horseshoes and stirrups. Nanny had put on a new Paisley shawl, and was counting the Things in her bag, which had been found in the basement just where she had left it.

'How smart you look, Nanny!' said Nollekens, giving her a hug. 'Let's be off. What are we waiting for?'

'The baby of course.'

'The baby? Is *he* going? But Nanny, he's too young!'

'Rubbish! Whose Christening is it, I'd like to know?'

'I wish it was mine,' said Nollekens. 'I'd be much better at it than he'll be. Why, he won't even be able to tell the Bishop his name. Will you?' he asked the baby, who was now brought in in the crisp robe and long lace veil. 'How is he, how is he?' Nollekens peeped under the veil. 'A trifle over-excited?'

'She's sleeping like a lamb,' said Mother Codling, laying the baby in its cradle till the time came. For she knew there was to be a surprise before they started; and here was Cookie coming in now (in her duffle cloak)[1] to give it to them. In her hand she carried an elegant white plaster vase, filled with an ivory flower-piece of silk and satin roses with silver leaves.

'Oh, Cookie, what have you got there?' cried Nollekens excitedly. 'What is it, what *is* it, what is it?'

'It's to go on top of the cake,' said Cookie grandly.

'Is it sweet?' Nollekens licked his finger to taste it.

'It's a nornament,' said Cookie, slapping his hand before he could mess up the beautiful vase. 'Now, Jen, draw the curtains, my girl!'

Jen pulled a cord that held together a pair of white muslin curtains trimmed with pink ribbons. They flew apart, revealing Cookie's enormous Christening-cake, sugar flower garden, sugar dovecote, sugar temple and all, and the white sugar cherubs standing on top with uplifted hands nearly touching the ceiling.

'Oo! Oo! Oo! Oo!' cried Abe and Sid and Dave and Hal.

'OO-OO!' cried Nollekens.

'It looks too good to cut,' said Megs.

'But it *will* be cut,' said Nollekens anxiously, 'won't it, Nanny? It will be, won't it, *won't* it?'

'There, there,' said Nanny, 'of course it will.'

'And I *can* have a piece, can't I? *Can't* I have a piece, Nanny?'

'If you're a very good boy.'

[1] She couldn't find it before because Mother Codling was using it as an ironing-blanket.

'*I* fetched the sugar to ice it,' boasted Abe.

'*I* fetched the almond paste,' chortled Sid.

'*I* fetched the currants and raisins,' crowed Dave.

'*I* fetched the candied cherries,' chuckled Hal.

'And *you* made the cake, I suppose,' sniffed Cookie. The cake was her masterpiece, and this was the proudest moment of her life. She mounted a chair and placed the vase of flowers on the upraised hands of the cherubs. 'There!' said Cookie.

'My mouth's fair watering,' said Mother Codling. She called across the room to Doll, 'Hurry up with your things, my girl. The sooner we're there the sooner we'll be back.'

'It's no use, mawther,' said Nollekens. 'Doll's not going.'

'*What's* that?' cried Mother Codling.

'Doll says she isn't going to the Christening.'

'Not going?' cried everybody. 'A mother not go to her own baby's Christening?'

'I never heard of such a thing,' said Nanny.

'Well, she *says* she isn't,' said Nollekens.

'Why not?' asked Nanny.

'Why not?' asked Mother Codling.

'Why not?' asked everybody.

'And she isn't giving the baby a present, either,' said Nollekens.

'A mother not give her own baby a present?' cried everybody.

'Why not?' asked Nanny.

'Why not?' asked Mother Codling.

'Why not?' demanded everybody, turning upon Doll as one man.

Doll sprang down from the window, her eyes running with tears. 'I'll tell you why not!' she sobbed. 'I'll tell you why not, why not! I'm not giving my baby a present, and I'm not going to the Christening, because——' She choked, and caught her breath.

'Because?' cried everybody.

'Because there isn't going to *be* a Christening,' whispered poor Doll.

'The girl's gone off her head,' said old Nan.

'Clean off it,' agreed everybody.

'No I've not then,' said Doll. 'It's the Christening that's off.'

Mother Codling shook her finger at her. 'How can you say so, darter, and your baby wearing the fine robe you spun for it yourself?'

'I didn't spin a thread of it,' said Doll.

'What!' cried everybody, wondering if their ears had heard aright.

'Who knows better than you that I can't spin?' said Doll to her mother. And turning to Nollekens she blurted out, 'Time you learned that I'm the worst spinster in Norfolk.'

'But—but—but—' stammered Nollekens. 'But what about the twelve skeins of flax you span in half an hour the very first time I ever saw you? She *did* spin twelve skeins of flax, didn't she, Nanny? You *said* she did, didn't you, mawther? And you were fair flummoxed by Doll's cleverness, wasn't she, Nanny?' Nollekens turned from one to the other in his bewilderment, and finally turned back to Doll. 'What about those twelve skeins you span?'

'It wasn't twelve skeins I'd spun,' whispered Doll, hanging her head, 'but twelve dumplings I'd eat.'

'Twelve dumplings!' gasped Nollekens. 'All in one go?'

Doll nodded, too ashamed to speak.

'Without—getting—a stomach-ache?'

Doll nodded again, and covered her face with her hands.

'Oh you wonderful, *wonderful* girl!' And Nollekens hugged Doll to his heart, bursting with admiration. He himself had once eaten twelve doughnuts when Cookie wasn't looking, and Nanny had given him a big dose of liquorice powder to stop the collywobbles. And now a *girl* had done what he couldn't do himself, and she was his wife! He hugged her so hard that Doll had hardly breath to murmur,

'Oh Nolly, if only I'd known! If only I'd known you'd like me for eating dumplings instead of spinning flax. I'd never have passed myself off for a spinster, if only I'd known.'

Then up spoke old Nan. 'But *somebody* spun the flax.'

And everybody demanded, 'Who *did* spin the flax?'

'A little black imp spun it, there!' said Doll.

'A little black *im*-P?' In his surprise, Nollekens practically spat the P into the Butler's eye.

'Last year and this he spun it,' said Doll, 'and today he's coming to be paid.'

'Let him come,' said Nollekens, pulling out his purse. 'We'll pay him.'

'Put that by,' said Doll. 'It's not money he's after. He bargained for something else.'

'Diamonds and pearls?' asked Mother Codling.

'Gold plate?' asked the Butler.

'A model railway,' suggested Nollekens, 'with points, and signals, and a ticket office, and——'

Doll stopped him, saying sadly, 'Me—and the baby.'

'*You*—and our *son*?' gasped Nollekens.

'The Queen! The Princess!' gasped everybody.

'Well, he jolly well won't get you,' spluttered Nollekens.

'He will,' said Doll. 'I promised. Else he wouldn't spin the flax.'

'Did you give him your solemn word of honour?' asked Nollekens.

Doll nodded as before.

'How *could* you?' said Nollekens.

Doll hung her head again and whispered, 'I was so afraid of——'

'Of what, Dollikins?'

'Your temper, Nollekens.'

'Oh!' said Nollekens. 'What a horrid person I must be.' And now it was he who hung his head.

'You can't help it,' said Doll gently, 'it's just your double nature.'

'Of *course* I can help it!' cried Nollekens indignantly. 'I'll give *up* my double nature. I'll never, never, never ask you to spin again. Never!'

157

'Oh,' sighed Doll, 'how lovely it would have been.'

'*Would* have been, Dollikins?'

'It's too late, it's too late,' cried Doll, wringing her hands. 'I gave my word of honour.'

'When is this imp coming?' asked Nollekens fiercely.

'Any minute now.'

'Then there's no time to lose!'

Nollekens snatched up the muffin-bell excitedly, and rushed from corner to corner of the room shouting, 'Muster the Guards! Man the Navy! Summon the Police! Send for the Fire Brigade! Fetch pistols—and pitchforks—and pikes—and penknives! Bar windows! bolt doors! block chimneys! stuff up keyholes! Don't leave a nook or a cranny that an imp can creep in at!'

'*He-he-he! He-he-he!*'

CHAPTER XX

Little Black Imp!

EVERYBODY stopped locking doors, shooting bolts, drawing blinds, and stopping up keyholes. The Nursery was in darkness. Where did this horrid little chuckle come from that froze the marrow in their bones?

'*He-he-he! He-he-he!*'

The vase on top of the Christening-cake began to glow as bright as fire, and out of it, like a live coal, popped the most hideous little black imp they had ever set eyes on. For one moment he perched cross-legged on the artificial flowers, then he leaped down to the floor, twirling his tail.

'Here I be! here I be!'

'*Who* be you?' demanded Nollekens. He pulled back the window-curtains so that he could have a good look at the interloper. 'Who be *you*?'

'That'd be telling,' grinned the Imp.

'And why not, if you've got a name to tell?'

'That's it in a nutshell,' said Doll. 'He's got a name, and if only we knew what it was his power would be broken. Three guesses we've got, and no more, to break his power.'

Nollekens brightened up. 'Three guesses? Pooh, one can guess anything in three. His name is——'

'Not so fast!' implored Doll. 'If you don't guess right you must give him your baby and me.'

'Yar pretty little baby!' crowed the Imp. 'Yar buxom little wife!'

He stooped over the cradle and grabbed at the baby's veil; so certain was he that nobody would guess his name in three, or three times three, or three times that.

The women rushed round the cradle to protect it. 'Hands off!' cried old Nan; and he edged away a little under her eye, because she was the sort of Nanny that even imps aren't quite comfortable with. Meanwhile, Nollekens was fumbling in all his pockets.

'Give you my baby? Give you my Doll? Anything —anything—anything but that!' He rushed up to the Imp saying, 'Look here! Here's my crown! Here's my sceptre! Here's my penknife with three blades! Take them and begone, you little black Imp!'

The Imp sneered at the crown, jeered at the sceptre, fleered at the penknife, and twirled his twirly tail.

'I—will—*not!* I—will—*not!* As sure as my name
is——'

'What?' cried everybody.

'As sure as my name is Never-mind-what!' jeered
the Imp.

Then Jen came running up and knelt before him.
'I'll give you my bunch of ribbons and my silver
fourpenny-bit,' said she, 'if you'll go back home, you
little black Imp, and stay there.'

The Imp sneered at the ribbons, jeered at the fourpenny-bit, twirled his twirly tail, and said, 'I—will—
not!'

Up stumped Cookie, with a copper saucepan in one
hand and a wooden spoon in the other. 'Here you
are, then!' said she. 'My very best saucepan and my
next-best wooden spoon. Take 'em and turn tail, you
little black Imp, as quick as winking.'

The Imp jeered at the saucepan, and fleered at the
spoon, twirled his twirly tail, and said, 'I—will—*not!*'

Along came the Butler. 'Well then,' said he, 'here's
my patent corkscrew and a jorum of champagne.
They're yours, you little black Imp, if you'll just be
off and never come back.'

The Imp fleered at the corkscrew and sneered at the
jorum, twirled his twirly tail, and said, 'I—will—*not!*'

'Look here then,' said Megs. 'What d'you say to
my hickory butter-pats and this nice bowl of curds and
whey? Just make yourself scarce with 'em, you little
black Imp, for ever and a day.'

But the Imp sneered at the butter-pats and jeered at

the curds, twirled his twirly tail, and said, 'I—will—
not!'

Next came the Gardener. 'Be sensible, do, for here's
my own spade, my own trowel, and my own potato-
prong, than which there's none better in Norfolk.
Pack up and make tracks, you little black Imp, and
good riddance!'

But the Imp jeered and sneered and fleered at the
spade, the trowel, and the prong, and twirled his
twirly tail. 'I—will—*not!*'

'Drat it!' cried Mother Codling coming forward,
'you can have my Grandad's Toby jug and my
Grannie's brass thimble, you little black Imp, if you'll
only take yourself off, you and your ugly mug.'

But he sneered and he jeered and he twirled his
twirly tail, and said, 'I—will—*not!*'

Next came Abe and Sid and Dave and Hal, carrying
big bags on their shoulders.

'A bag of lime!' said Abe.

'A bushel of barley!' said Sid.

'Another of oats!' said Dave.

'And another of best manure!' said Hal.

'Good measure!' they cried together; 'so cut your
stick in double-quick time, you little black Imp!'

He sneered and he jeered and he twirled his twirly
tail, and said, 'I—will—*not!*'

Last of all came old Nan, with nothing in her hands
but her own clenched fists.

'What'll *yew* give me, then?' asked the Imp, edging
away a bit.

'I'll give you a clout on your lug, lad,' said Nan fiercely, 'and another one on your behind. Be off, you little black Imp, if you don't want me to give you What For!'

'Be off, be off,' cried everybody, 'if you don't want What For.'

But the Imp only sneered, and jeered, and fleered, and twirled his twirly tail faster than ever.

'I—will—*not!*' said he. 'I—will—*not!* As sure as my name is——'

'WHAT?' shouted everybody. 'As sure as your name is WHAT?'

'As sure as my name is Never-mind-what!' chuckled the Imp. And he twirled himself up to the window-seat, where Doll was gazing into the distance with all her eyes.

CHAPTER XXI

The Last Three Guesses

'TIME's up, Doll Codling,' said the Spindle-Imp. 'Guess my name!'

'I want my little sister,' whispered Doll. 'Where's Poll, oh where is Poll?'

'Whar yew'll niver see her no more,' chuckled the Imp. He pointed at the crowd of people standing with their rejected presents in their hands. 'Guess my name!' he cried mockingly.

'Don't rush us!' said Nollekens, in an annoyed voice. He walked up and down, tapping his head for an idea, while the rest went into a huddle round Doll at the window, and consulted in whispers.

'What do you think?' asked Mother Codling.

'What do *you* think?' asked the Butler.

'I fancy Nicodemus myself,' said Mother Codling.

'He isn't Nicodemus,' said Doll. 'I tried that yesterday, and it wasn't right.'

'What about Zebedee?' suggested Cookie.

'I tried Zebedee,' said Doll, 'and it was wrong.'

'Did you try Hasdrubal?' asked Megs.

'That isn't Hasdrubal,' said Doll.

At this they scratched their heads and tried to think some more, but none of them was used to thinking much, and they didn't find it easy. Suddenly Nollekens, who had been doing his thinking all by himself,

164

pointed a triumphant finger at the Imp, crying, 'Your name is Sophonisba!'

> *He, he, he!*   (chuckled the Imp)
> *Thar goos one!*
> *Doll will be mine*
> *Time yew've done!*

'Oh you, booby!' exclaimed Mother Codling. 'Sophonisba, forsooth!'

'Sophonisba's a feminine name,' said Cookie.

'And if it is?' said Nollekens.

'That there's a man,' said the Gardener. 'Leastways, that's no female.'

'Why didn't somebody *tell* me?' pouted Nollekens.

'There you go, that's you all over,' scolded Nan. 'Rushing at it like a bull at a scarlet tablecloth, messing up one of our precious chances.'

'We've got two left,' said Nollekens sulkily. 'One can guess anything in two.'

'As long as you keep your mouth shut,' said Nan.

Nollekens laid his finger on his lips as a sort of promise to be good, and back they went into their huddle with their heads together.

The Gardener thought, 'Methusalem's likely.'

'So *I* thought,' said Doll, 'but I thought wrong.'

'In my opinion,' said the Butler, 'Nebuchadnezzar.'

'Then you must change your opinion,' said Doll.

'He looks like Mark to me,' said Abe.

'Nay, Sammle,' said Sid.

'Nay, Bill,' said Dave.

'Nay, Ned,' said Hal.

But Doll shook her head. 'I tried all those, in vain.'

This brought them again to the end of their thinking. The men scratched their heads, the women thumped their brows, some with their eyes on the floor, and the rest with their eyes on the ceiling. Seeing his chance, Nollekens slipped out of their midst, and dashed back to the Imp.

'Your name is Esmeralda!' he cried.

> *He, he, he!*   (chuckled the Imp)
> *Thar goos two!*
> *One more fault*
> *And all's up wi' yew!*

'Esmeralda, *Esmeralda*!' scolded Nan, shaking her fist at Nollekens. 'I could skin you!'

Nollekens kicked his heels. 'Why *shouldn't* it be Esmeralda?'

'Have you no eyes in your head?' demanded Nanny. 'That imp of mischief is masculine.'

'You might have mentioned it,' said Nollekens.

'Poll, oh, Poll, where are you?' whispered Doll, wringing her hands. One by one her precious chances slipped from her. The others too were beginning to despair. They muttered in each other's ears: 'I've got it! that's——' And, 'Nay, I'm certain that's——' And 'Take my word for it, that's——'

Once more Nollekens sneaked away towards the Imp, quite sure he had got it this time. 'Your name,' he said in a loud whisper, 'is——'

'STOP HIM!' bawled Mother Codling.

Before Nollekens could squander their last chance the Butler had collared him, and clapped a hand over his mouth. Nanny waddled up with her severest look on her round apple-face.

'Go and stand in the corner!' she commanded. 'Go on!' Nollekens didn't like it; but he went.

The Imp watched him maliciously, and Nollekens knew he was jeering at him, as one boy who has escaped will jeer at another boy who has been caught. '*I'll* show him!' thought Nollekens. 'I'll show 'em all, you see if I don't!'

They weren't paying any attention to him now. He could hear them muttering and spluttering, each trying to get his suggestion in ahead of the rest. 'Now if you ask *me*——' said Cookie. 'Nobody's asking you!' snapped Nan. 'Listen, mawther——' muttered Abe. 'Listen, mawther—— Listen, mawther——' muttered Sid and Dave. 'Listen, mawther——' piped Hal. 'Quiet, the lot of you!' said Mother Codling. 'Listen to *me*——'

But chancing to look round, she caught the Imp capering like a mischievous urchin, daring Nolly to play truant from his corner; and Nolly was stealing towards him, like a needle to a magnet.

'STOP HIM!'

Round and round the room they chased the truant, and tripped him up, and gagged his mouth with Abe's red and green necktie, before he could say another word. The gleeful Imp, seeing his triumph at hand,

167

continued to caper in their midst, crying, 'D'yew give it up? D'yew give it up?'

'Of course we don't give it up!' snapped Nan.

'Then guess me now or guess me niver!' crowed the Imp.

'Another minute,' begged Mother Codling. 'For mercy's sake, another minute to think in!'

'Not another minute more,' snarled the Imp. 'Time's up!' He made a grab at the baby in the cradle.

For the last time Doll, all hope gone, moaned, 'Poll, Poll, Poll, where are you?'

The window was pulled wide open and there on the sill stood Poll, her ugly disguise all torn, her face all stained, her hair all loose, her breath all but gone, after her long run. She had just enough left to gasp, in a fierce whisper:

'*Nimmy-nimmy-not!*'

The Imp shrank and shrivelled under the glare in her eyes. 'Runton!' he muttered.

CHAPTER XXII

'Nimmy-Nimmy-Not!'

POLL swung her tired legs slowly over the sill, and dropped into the room. She was feeling very wobbly as she advanced step by step on the Imp. Only an hour or two ago he had been standing over her in the Witching-Wood, jeering at her helplessness; but now, as he crouched before her, he knew the game was up.

'Nimmy-nimmy-not!' said Poll again, 'your name is——'

Then she saw the baby, their precious baby, clutched in the Imp's black skinny arms, and all her tiredness left her as she sprang upon him.

'*You leave our baby be!*' cried Poll, snatching the baby out of his grasp, and pointing her finger at him she declared fiercely:

> *Nimmy-nimmy-not!*
> *Your name is Tom Tit Tot!*

Tom Tit Tot covered his face with his hands, and yowled.

Then Nollekens took up his part in the guessing-game, which Poll had just won for them. Pointing *his* finger he repeated, for all the world as though he was the successful guesser:

> *Nimmy-nimmy-not!*
> *Your name is Tom Tit Tot!*

170

'Tom Tit Tot!' cried everybody, in their loudest voices. 'Tom Tit Tot! Nimmy-nimmy-not, your name is

Tom

Tit

Tot!'

Each time his name was uttered the Imp crouched lower, and yowled more dreadfully. Nan and Mother Codling, Cookie, Megs, and Jen advanced on him from one side; the Butler, the Gardener, Abe and Sid and Dave and Hal closed in on the other. If they had got hold of him his life wouldn't have been worth a moment's purchase.

Before they could do so, there was a bang and a flash and a fizzle, and the Spindle-Imp disappeared out of their lives for evermore. Only a little black smudge was left to show where he had cowered on the carpet.

And beside it, Poll, all her fierceness gone, sat rocking the baby to and fro in her arms, sobbing,

'Hullo . . . I'm your aunt.'

CHAPTER XXIII

Fairy Caskets

'STOP blubbing, silly,' said Mother Codling.

It seemed to Poll she would never stop blubbing again, so choked was she with all sorts of feelings she couldn't have explained if she'd tried. Even when Doll stooped to take the baby from her she held it tighter, as though only by holding it herself could she be sure it was safe.

Things were happening all round her in the nursery. The interrupted Christening had begun to go on just where it had left off, for when the worst is over the best sets in again. The air was throbbing with the music of the church bells, which had been muffled while the baby was in danger. At the same time the palace front-door-bell was clanging noisily. Jen peeped out of the window, cried 'Visitors!' and hurried into the passage.

'What sort?' shouted Nollekens.

'Very grand ones,' called Jen. 'They've got their wings on.' And she flew downstairs to let them in as though she had wings herself.

'It's the Godmothers!' said Nollekens excitedly. 'Is my crown on straight, Nanny?'

Everybody hustled and bustled to make the best of themselves before the guests were announced. The

Butler stood to attention at the door, Noll went and sat on his throne, and Doll held out her arms once more for the baby.

'Stop blubbing, can't ye?' repeated Mother Codling. 'The Fairy Godmothers have come agen. And look at ye, do! All tattered and torn like a scarecrow in a cornfield! What *will* the fairies think of you?'

Poll let Mother Codling take the baby from her and give it to Doll, who cuddled it as only a mother can, though aunts can be quite good at it, as I happen to know. Then Cookie hastened with a wet sponge and towel to wipe the tear-stains off the little girl's face, and Mother Codling came back with a brush and comb and tidied her hair. It's wonderful what a lot can be done while the guests are coming up a flight of stairs. Poll was all ready just as the Butler announced:

'The Morning Fairy!'

In came the First Godmother like the rosy dawn, bearing in her hands a ruby casket. Abe escorted the Morning Fairy to the throne, where she kissed the baby, and laid the casket on Doll's knee.

'What's inside it?' asked Nollekens.

'The gift of a kind heart,' said the Morning Fairy.

'Oh,' said Nollekens. 'Well, it's very nice of you, anyhow.'

The Morning Fairy gave the baby her blessing, and stood aside as the Butler announced:

'The Noontide Fairy!'

The Second Godmother filled the nursery with sunlight as she came in, carrying a golden casket. It was

Sid who escorted her proudly to the throne, where she too kissed the baby, and placed the casket on Doll's lap.

'Is there something in it?' asked Nollekens.

'Yes,' said the Noontide Fairy. 'The gift of gladness.'

'Oh,' said Nollekens. 'Well, I daresay it's what girls like.'

The Noontide Fairy blessed the baby, and took her place beside her rosy sister.

'The Twilight Fairy!' announced the Butler.

The Third Godmother was dressed in dusky blue, and she carried a sapphire casket. Dave hastened to conduct her to the foot of the throne.

'It isn't empty, is it?' asked Nollekens anxiously, as the Twilight Fairy, having kissed the baby, laid her casket with the other two.

'Far from it,' said the Twilight Fairy. 'It contains the gift of beauty.'

'Oh,' said Nollekens. 'I see. Well, I expect it's just what she wanted.'

The Twilight Fairy gave the baby *her* blessing, and after that nothing else happened.

'Is that *all*?' asked Nollekens.

'That is all,' said the Butler.

'But I invited four,' said Nollekens. 'Where is the Fourth Godmother?'

'There were but the three,' said Jen.

'I *did* ask four,' said Nollekens, 'didn't I, Nanny? And the fourth one *said* she'd be there. Where is the

Midnight Fairy? We can't have the Christening without her.'

'Oh, look!' whispered Poll.

All eyes followed hers, which were turned on the top of the cake. The beautiful ornament of flowers, which Tom Tit Tot had burst asunder when he leapt into the room, was once more in its place, gleaming like moonshine on the sea. Out of it rose a shape on silver wings, that everybody first thought was a bird, but when it floated down as light as a moonbeam, it was seen to be a lady of the most exquisite loveliness. In her hands she bore a silver casket.

Dazzled by her beauty, Hal stumbled forward to lead her to the throne; but she turned from him and floated straight to Poll, who gazed at her with great wonder, all the greater because the Midnight Fairy was no stranger. She knew immediately who it was.

'My Curlew,' murmured Poll, 'it's my Silver Curlew.'

The silver shape (lady or curlew who could say?) placed her casket in Poll's hands.

'For me?' whispered Poll.

'What's in it, what's in it?' called Nollekens.

The Silver Lady only smiled into Poll's eyes; but an answer came from the windowsill, in a voice which Poll heard with great wonder, all the greater because it was a voice she knew.

'Magic,' said the voice of Charlee Loon. 'There's magic in the casket, little Poll.'

He was standing there, no more in his fisherman's

rags, but like the lady dressed in shining clothes, and his eyes and voice were as bright and clear as stars. He held out his hand to the Midnight Fairy, saying, 'It's time to go home, lady, time to go home.'

It seemed to Poll that night had come again, as the Lady, or the Curlew (which was it *really?*) rose in the air, joined Charlee at the window, and spreading her wings flew with him into a sky that glittered with stars.

'Charlee! O—O Charlee!' cried Poll imploringly. 'Charlee, Charlee! are you the Man in the Moon?' . . .

'To Church, to Church!' commanded old Nan.

176

The Nursery was bright as day again, bonnets were being tied, nobody seemed to have noticed anything special but Poll.

The procession was formed, led by Noll and Doll with the baby. The Godmothers followed, with everybody else in order of precedence. Only Poll, who should have been in front, came last of all, rubbing her eyes and nursing her silver casket.

In Norwich Cathedral the baby was baptized and given the name of Joan.

CHAPTER XXIV

The Sea-Shell Sings

I T was all over.

The happy day had come to an end. The fears and dangers of the past year were forgotten. The Christening-cake had been cut, everybody had had a piece, they had taken hands and danced round it till they were tired, and had gone contented to bed.

Yes, it was all over. . . . *But was it?*——

In all the palace Poll only lay awake. Her silver

casket was under her pillow, where she could feel it with one hand. The other hand held her sea-shell to her ear. Through her open window the full moon sailed into view on the sapphire sea, where myriad stars twinkled like drops of music. The voice of the ocean in the distance seemed to accompany their voices, singing tunes and rhymes about everything that had been happening. At first Poll could not hear the words very clearly, but strange to say as she grew sleepier they came to her distinctly through the shell against her ear.

> *The Man in the Moon*
> *Came down too soon*
> *To ask his way to Norwich.*
> *He went to the south*
> *And burned his mouth*
> *By eating cold plum porridge.*

Every child in Norfolk knows that one. Poll had known it all her life. But tonight her shell was singing rhymes about the Man in the Moon that Poll had never heard before.

> *He hears the bells of Norwich Tower,*
> * He hears the big bells sing*
> *Like music ringing from a flower*
> * In Anglia in spring.*
> *The moony mountains have no song*
> *So bright and bold, so sweet and strong,*
> *The Man in the Moon must go along*
> * To find the bells that ring.*

What was happening up there in the moon? Wasn't that Charlee in his silver clothes, eager to jump down on the way to Norwich? And wasn't that the Midnight Fairy holding him back? What is the shell saying? . . .

> *The Lady in the Moon*
> *Says No, no, no!*
> *None but a loon*
> *Would go, go, go*
> *Away from the moon*
> *So far, far, far,*
> *To listen to a tune*
> *On another star.*

But she pleaded in vain. The bells of Norwich were drawing him down to earth, and the shell was singing for the Lady again. . . .

> *'If you will go, honey,*
> *Then I will go too,*
> *I cannot stay lonely*
> *And longing for you;*
> *But whatever we find*
> *On the Anglian plain,*
> *We shall lose ourselves, honey,*
> *Till both come again.'*

> *Down he falls,*
> *Down he falls,*
> *Falls down the wind,*
> *He loses his wits*
> *And he leaves them behind.*

The Sea-Shell Sings

Down she flies,
Down she flies
Swift as a word.
She loses her shape
And comes down like a bird.

He finds the Tower of Norwich
Beyond the Norfolk sands,
The moon that gave him birth is gone
Among the distant lands,
He fishes in strange waters,
He walks an alien plain,
He looks upon the distant moon
And longs to come again.

'We'll come again, honey,
When all has been done,
When spindle is idle
And story is spun.
It may not be long,
Though it may not be soon,
Till we find ourselves, honey,
Come back to the moon.'

Oh, what is happening? Poll's drowsy thoughts are spinning all sorts of things in a bit of a muddle, like a tangled skein of wool: a tangle of dumplings and ducks-eggs, of wedding-bells and Christening-bells, of a witch in a wood and a fairy with a casket, of a spindle and a fishing-boat, of Doll crying and a baby crowing, of a curlew in a cage and the curlew flying . . . of a

shell speaking in her ear with the voice of Charlee
Loon: '*Once upon a time was a man in the moon . . . and
once upon the same time was a lady in the moon . . . the
moon was a wondrous place, more wondrous than the world . . .
but one fine night . . .*'

> *Up he goes!*
> *Up he goes!*
> *Upward he flits,*
> *Up in the moonshine*
> *He finds his lost wits.*
> *Up flies the Lady*
> *To heaven's white pearl—*
> *She came down a bird*
> *And she goes up a girl.*

'O—O Charlee! O my Silver Curlew!' Is it all
over? Listen! the shell is singing its last song. . . .

> *The Moon, the lovely Moon,*
> *When the town's asleep*
> *In all her silver beauty*
> *Wanders down the steep,*
> *Wanders down the steep*
> *Unseen by you and me*
> *In all her silver beauty*
> *To walk upon the sea.*

No, spin Poll's thoughts, not all over, never quite
over, come again, come again, it'll come again in half
an hour. . . .

She has gone to sleep.